Cosmic Chaos

By

C.L. Roth

Carol Englehaupt
2370 E. 2649 Rd.
815-357-1401
Carolenglehaupt@gmail.com

ISBN: 978-0-9846619-6-1
Interior design by Booknook.biz.

Cosmic Chaos

ACKNOWLEDGEMENTS

The story starts in the mind of the writer but its growth depends on many people.

I owe thanks and gratitude to: Holly Lisles http://hollyl-isle.com/ Without Holly's classes, especially her How to Think Sideways class, I would not be able to finish a story. Her generosity in sharing her knowledge and experience is a true gift.

Marion Sipes of Dreamspring Designs http://marionsipe. blogspot.com/ for her beautiful cover art.

My thanks to Liz Schroeder. It takes a special person to edit my writing and keep me on track. I tend to wander and it takes a talented person to keep me focused.

Thank you to Silver Jay Media http://silverjaymedia.com/ services/ for proofreading the manuscript. I freely admit I'm comma-challenged. In addition, he brought up story elements that made me think. I have a better story for his guidance and input.

http://www.booknook.biz/ for the digital conversions. My thanks and gratitude.

Rebecca Rowe http://www.redjasperartistry.com/ for her beautiful photography. She went above and beyond in her creativity in catching acceptable images. The camera is not my friend but Becky is.

I owe special thanks to the 5th, 6th, 7th, and 8th graders at Dwight Elementary school. Mrs. Goley has my gratitude for introducing her students to my books. The children give me valuable feedback, suggestions, and encouragement.

A special thank you to my grandchildren. They hold a big chunk of my heart and I'm thrilled they are finally old enough to read my books. Thank you, Jackson, Jefferson, Charles, and Isla.

Chapter 1

A whisper of sound woke him. Soft creaks, sliding footsteps, then a muffled curse hastily swallowed. Bo Tanner raised his head from his pillow and strained to see through the pre-dawn gloom. What he saw brought him bolt upright in bed.

"What are you doing?" Bo blinked to clear his eyes and wished his brain would wake up.

The dark figure crawling through the open window jerked upright, cracking his head on the window frame. "Geez, scare a guy, will you?" Mark Cooper pulled himself back into the room and stood up. "I'm sorry I woke you up."

Bo untangled himself from the sheet. His cousin, Mark, had given up the guest bedroom to Flicker, a Hunter from the magical realms. Renegades, escapees from a magical world, had opened a hole in the sky intending to escape from the Hunters by hiding on Earth. Cosmos, leader of the Hunters, was off hunting for Hemlock and Dalt, the two renegades still at large.

Silas had taken Dragen, leader of the Renegades and the boy, Ian, back to their world to atone for the crimes they committed. He would return with volunteers to help Earth adapt to the changing environment.

In the two weeks Silas had been gone, Mark had grown increasingly morose and quiet. Anger stirred in Bo. "Were you going to take off without telling me? After everything we've been through this summer?"

"I'm sorry." Mark stumbled back to the bed and sat down. "I was hoping to be well on the road before you woke up. I had trouble getting the screen out of the window in the dark."

Bo ran a hand over his unruly hair. "Shouldn't you talk to Dad about this? Don't you think he's worried, too?"

Mark sat hunched over, silent for so long Bo feared he wouldn't speak at all. When the rush of words spilled out, Bo feared he'd never stop. "I need to go, Bo. I was afraid Uncle Ed would pat me on the head and make me stay here. After what we went through six weeks ago, I think I have a right to go after my parents. We fought the baddest dude in the world. And we won."

"Not alone." Bo reminded him. "We had Hunters on our side, remember?"

"I remember." Mark sounded grim. "But we handled ourselves. We didn't panic. We did what we needed to do. Mom and Dad were due here five days ago. I'm worried."

Mark's voice quivered on those last two words and Bo felt a pang of sympathy. He worried, too. When the rip in the sky spewed renegades, cosmic hunters, and magic into Earth's atmosphere, Uncle Harley showed up bearing letters from Mark's parents. Bo's Uncle Frank and Aunt Claire wanted Mark to stay here where they planned on joining him.

Mark's mother sent him words of love and reassurance. His father, a forest ranger, sent survival techniques and warnings. The catastrophic rip in the sky spilling alien air into Earth's atmosphere had set off a chain reaction that would eventually change the world. And it all started at Grayson, Missouri, Mark's home town.

"They should be here." Mark spoke so softly Bo almost didn't hear him. "I can feel in my bones something is wrong. I already tossed the duffle bag through the window."

In the dim light, Bo could see enough of Mark's face to know he wasn't going to be able to reason with Mark. "Wait a minute. I'll pull some clothes on."

"You're not going with me," Mark argued. "Your dad needs you here."

"He needs you, too." Bo reached for the shorts lying on the floor by the bed, hesitated before going to the dresser for a pair of jeans. Shorts would be cooler in the hot July weather but jeans would give his legs more protection. "Have you forgotten the hag, Hemlock, and Dalt are still in the area? Eden needs watched over."

"Flicker can do that." Mark sounded certain of that.

Bo agreed. Flicker, the girl from the other world, possessed remarkable skills and training.

Mark added, "Eden isn't a pushover. If she ever gets over her fear of using magic she'll be a powerhouse. I wouldn't want to mess with her."

"Yeah," Bo agreed. He pulled on his sneakers and stood up. "That's Flicker's job. She's supposed to teach all of us how to use magic. She said the change, because we're so close to the center, will happen fast."

Silence again. Bo, on his way to the bedroom door, stopped and waited.

Mark took a few steps toward him, then stopped again. Bo couldn't make out his face clearly enough to identify the expression but he heard anguish in his voice. "I don't think I'll be able to make the change."

"What do you mean?" Bo felt bewildered. "Flicker said we're young enough. Our brains are still young enough to be flexible. We can learn to use magic."

"I can't explain it." Mark sounded exasperated. "I just worry, okay? And why are we going through the door? The window is unscreened now."

Bo hurried to the window and struggled to put the screen in place. He could tell by the feel that it was wrong. He shut the window to keep out bugs and mosquitos, then hurried back to the bedroom door.

"I'm awake now. You don't have to go through the window. Have you seen how far off the ground it is? We'll sneak through the kitchen and be on our way. I'll walk with you for a while."

Mark didn't reply but he followed Bo through the dark kitchen. Bo knew from experience his parents would be up soon. If Mark wanted to leave they'd better hurry. The early morning air, even in the midst of July, felt cool and humid. Sleepy robins chirped for dawn.

The two boys crept along the side of the house to Bo's bedroom window.

***

"Didn't you say you dropped the duffle bag out the window?" Bo whispered to Mark.

"I did. Straight out the window." Mark stood at Bo's shoulder. He struggled to see through the gloom. "I'm usually glad I don't see the sunrise in the morning but this morning I'm wishing for a little more light. Where could the bag be?"

The two boys felt around. Bo straightened up and stood, shoulder to shoulder, by Mark. "I don't think it's here. What do you think happened to it? Did you think you tossed it and it's still inside the bedroom?"

Mark gave Bo a look that would have shriveled him if he could have seen it clearly. A dark man-shaped shadow, bigger than they were, loomed up behind them. A hard hand gripped Mark's shoulder.

"Dalt!" Mark shouted. He let fly a hard elbow punch. The dark figure 'oomphed' and let loose with some masterful swearing.

"Not Dalt, you fool. It's me. Harley."

Bo didn't know whether to laugh or howl. Uncle Harley had scared him to his toes but seeing Mark hit him with a well-placed elbow to the solar plexus was funny. Listening to his uncle swear and moan, he decided silence would serve him best.

"I've got your duffle bag, boy. We need to talk. Now get your fanny into the kitchen."

Neither boy dared to speak. Harley's tone of voice scared Bo. He'd been in trouble a lot but this felt different. He wasn't sure why. They stepped through the kitchen doorway. His father stood by the counter putting the globe back on the kerosene lamp.

Bo sighed and leaned closer to Mark to whisper. "We're in for it now."

Chapter 2

Bo's stomach sank even lower at the sight of his father moving to the kitchen stove to put a pot of water on to boil for coffee. The kitchen was his mother's domain. Thank goodness the stove worked on gas and not electricity. The strange effect magic had on motors and electricity didn't seem to bother the gas stove.

"Let me do that." Bo's mother, Grace, hurried into the kitchen and gently pushed Ed out of the way. "You go sit down and talk to the boys."

Ed kissed his wife on the cheek, sharing a deep gaze with her before turning to look at the boys. Bo felt his stomach shrivel at his father's grim expression and glacial eyes. Ed jerked his chin toward the kitchen table.

Bo didn't need to be told twice. He slid onto a kitchen chair, folded his hands in his lap, and waited for his father to start yelling.

Mark slid onto the chair next to him. Uncle Harley sat down opposite Ed. The old man looked tired and Bo wondered if he'd been up all night waiting for Mark to make a break for Grayson. He wouldn't put it past his uncle to know their every plan. Bo knew the old man had left home at age 14, Bo's own age as of two weeks ago. Mark would turn 14 in November.

The smell of fresh-brewed coffee permeated the kitchen followed by the sizzle of bacon hitting a hot skillet. He watched his mother mix up biscuit dough, a sight that almost made him glad their life had gotten harder. He loved the home-cooked meals his mother was now forced to make.

Ed smiled at Grace when she placed a mug of hot coffee in front of him. She handed a second mug to Harley. Bo waited in misery while his dad sipped the hot drink. He'd rather get the yelling over with. Then maybe he could enjoy eating breakfast without his stomach feeling like a leaden lump.

"I wasn't going anywhere," he burst out, unable to stand the silence any longer. "I only- -

He stopped and fell silent when Ed held up his hand.

Ed glanced briefly at Harley. "You were right. I knew Mark was worried but I didn't see him making a break for Grayson. I thought he'd wait."

Harley grunted. "I recognized the signs. The boy takes after me. I knew he wasn't going to be patient very long."

Ed nodded and turned thoughtful eyes on his nephew. "I know you think I'm angry with you, but I'm not. I'm worried, too. I love my sister and she's married to a good man. Your father knows better than we do how to handle a catastrophic emergency. The problem is, we have information he doesn't. We have Flicker and Cosmos. Silas will be back as soon as he can. We know what that rip in the sky was and what it's doing to our world. That's information he needs."

Ed took another sip of coffee. Bo could tell his dad was gathering his thoughts. He smiled at his mother when she placed steaming cups of hot chocolate in front of him and Mark. The powdered milk didn't taste so bad when chocolate syrup was added to it.

Ed tensed, and a sharp curse, hastily smothered, burst from him. "I hate this waiting. I want to take off and go get them." He slammed his coffee cup on the table.

Bo's stomach clenched even tighter at the unguarded anguish on his father's face.

"The problem is, I can't go. We're going to need all the food I can grow. I need to be here taking care of the farm and your mother. When people panic and start to run, and they will..." Ed shot a hard look at Harley. The old man nodded in agreement.

"When that happens, I need to be here to protect our animals and our property. We're off the main route and our road is a dead-end so we're not apt to have people wander by but when winter starts to close in and food gets scarce we're going to have to watch for thieves. Or worse," Ed added, his voice soft and low. "I can't go." Ed shot another hard look at Mark. "I know you think I'm going to try to talk you into staying here. Or maybe order you to stay here. But I'm not."

Mark's eyes widened and he shot Bo a look of amazement. Then he turned back to his uncle and listened with fierce concentration.

"I think someone needs to go assess what's going on. Help if help is needed. But I don't agree you should go alone."

Grace stopped in the process of pulling the pan of biscuits out of the oven. "Oh, Ed. No."

He stood up, walked to her side. Took the pot holder from her hands and removed the pan from the oven. He busied himself at the stove, sliding food around and turning off burners. Then he put a gentle arm around her shoulders and led her to the table.

"Sit, Grace. You need to hear this too."

Bo could tell Grace wished she could be anywhere else but the kitchen table. His mother sat down and Ed refilled his coffee cup, topped off Harley's, and offered a cup to Grace. She shook her head. He sat down and looked at Mark, examining the boy with hard eyes.

"I saw how you handled yourself when the Hunters captured Dragen and his followers. But what you're going into now is far different. We can plan for this. And you'll need supplies. I don't want you traveling alone."

"Not Bo," Grace choked out. "Please, Ed."

"Not Bo alone." Ed reached over and put his hand on top of his wife's, giving her hand a gentle squeeze. "We'll put Harley in charge. The boys can go with him."

"No," a new voice, light and lilting, answered him. Flicker entered the kitchen. Small-boned, delicate and frail in appearance, she looked deceptively innocent.

Flicker had been left behind to protect Eden from the dimensional renegades still at large. She'd been given the second job of teaching the children when they could use magic, how to use magic, and most importantly, when not to use magic; it seemed a big job for one small woman.

Cosmos was in pursuit of Hemlock and Dalt. Silas had warned the family that Hemlock would be watching for ways to gain control of Bo's little sister Eden. Much to the surprise of the other-worlders, Eden proved to be something they had never seen before: a human focus that drew magic to her like a sponge soaks up water.

"We need the boys to help watch Eden. We need more eyes on the girl, not fewer." Flicker quivered in indignation.

Ed frowned and gazed into his coffee cup. Grace rose and started putting plates and food on the kitchen table. Bo's stomach growled.

Flicker strengthened her argument. "The children haven't even begun to learn how to use magic effectively. I need as much time with them as I can get."

Bo didn't like the smile that tilted the corners of Ed's mouth up. His father raised the cup to his lips and looked at Flicker over the rim. "Then I guess you'd better plan on going with them."

"Ed, no." Grace put the bowl of scrambled eggs on the table before it could slip out of her hands. "If Flicker goes, that means Eden has to go with her. You can't do that."

"We have to, Grace." Sadness darkened Ed's eyes. "I agree with Mark. I can feel in my bones that Claire and Frank need help. Harley and Mark have to go to Grayson. And if Mark goes, Bo needs to go. Flicker can't watch the girls by herself."

'Remember this," Flicker added. "By heading into Grayson we're stronger than anybody else. The magic has already taken over. Eden is perhaps the strongest wielder of magic in the area right now. Nobody can overpower her once she learns how to protect herself. I am working on defense and attack with her now."

"Is she learning? Really learning?" Grace leaned toward the younger woman. "I know what Cosmos's judgment of her did to her. She has nightmares, Flicker. She needs me. She's just a little girl."

Flicker started to speak and stopped. She looked at Ed and shrugged. "I admit Eden has doubts but she still has power. Maybe taking her into the center of magic will show her better than I can teach her when and how to use her power."

"And maybe it won't," Grace choked and hurried back to the stove to plate the bacon and sausage.

Ed frowned, worry turning his blue eyes almost black. "What do you think, Harley? Can you get the children to Grayson safely?"

The old man nodded. "Yes, but it's a fifty mile walk. I could do that in two, maybe three days. With Eden along it will take longer than that. Five days if we do ten miles a day."

"I can spare the pony." He ignored Bo's protest. They all knew Bo and the pony, Teddy, didn't get along. But Eden loved the little brown beast and the pony loved her. Putting Eden on Teddy would speed the walk considerably.

Grace, the picture of mutinous anger, put the last of the food on the table. "I'm against this whole plan, sending my babies into a danger zone. But if you're set on doing this…" She shot an apologetic look toward Mark. "I'm sorry, honey. I love Claire and Frank too, I just worry about you children being put in danger.

"Anyway." She turned back to Ed. "If you're determined this is what has to happen, have you considered making a trade with the Nelsons? They breed and raise horses. Maybe they will loan some out to us in exchange for a cow. Meat is going to be very scarce this winter. We have forty head of steers that were due to be shipped out this fall. It won't hurt to ask, will it?"

Ed nodded. "That's a good idea, Grace. Using horses would shorten the five-day trip, maybe even allow them to make it in two."

He looked at Mark. "Will you wait, Mark? Give me twenty-four hours to pull together a working plan for you?"

"Yes, sir." Mark leaped to his feet and went to his uncle. He grabbed him in a big hug, continued to Grace. "Thank you, Aunt Grace."

Bo's mother pulled her nephew into her arms and hugged him tightly. Tears glistened on her cheeks. Bo knew how much the trip to Grayson meant to Mark when his cousin stood wrapped in his mother's arms and cried.

Chapter 3

"Bo, come outside and see." Eden, her blond curls flying, came rushing up to grab his hand and pull him toward the kitchen door.

Bo pulled back. "Don't rush me, midget. What are we going outside to see?"

His little sister grinned, her blue eyes full of laughter. "Come with me, Bo. Mark is already out there. Mr. Nelson is here and you should see what he brought."

Eden dropped his hand and darted out the door. Bo picked up the biscuit-and-bacon sandwich he'd made from the leftover breakfast and followed his little sister. He wished he could share Eden's enthusiasm but, no matter how he looked at it, whatever Mr. Nelson brought would turn out to be Teddy times four.

Sure enough, Bo sighed, and gulped half the biscuit sandwich in one bite. Mr. Nelson, sitting atop a big black gelding and leading three more horses, came trotting down the driveway toward the barn.

Eden and Shelly were enraptured. Shelly jumped up and down clapping her hands and squealing. Mark eyed the horses with shrewd eyes, seeing them as his way home.

Bo shoved the rest of the sandwich into his mouth and heard Harley say, "It can't be any different from riding the motorcycle."

Oh, yes it can, Bo thought to himself. *A motorcycle doesn't decide to do things you don't tell it to.*

Brand Nelson dismounted in front of Ed and Harley. "I'll give you the use of four horses for however long you need them. If one of them gets injured or killed you replace it with a cow, preferably a bred cow. I'll trade the use of the horses for one steer that we butcher in the fall. Since I don't know how to do that and we have no way to get the animal to the locker, I'll need you and Harley to show us how it's done."

Ed nodded. "Thank you, Brand. I appreciate this. I hope you brought us older horses and not your show stock."

Brand grinned, teeth shining white in his darkly-tanned face. "All of my horses are show stock. But I brought horses that are pleasure-trained and not the performance horses. You don't need speed and agility on this trip. The pleasure-trained horses are steady on the trail."

***

Obedient. Bo stood up and spat dirt out of his mouth. *Well-trained.* He swatted at the grime on the knees of his pants. Of them all, he was the only one the horses hated. He said so out loud.

"They don't hate you," Shelly scolded him. "They don't even know you and you're not mean to them. You did everything Mr. Nelson told you to."

Bo glared at his sister. "If they don't hate me, why do they pick on me? I've ridden three horses. The brown one took me to the fence corner and stood there with his face in the corner and ignored everything I told him to do. I thought the paint horse was nice until he jumped half-way across the corral, spooking at something nobody could see. He jumped right out from under me. I know what it feels like to sit suspended in air. And the landing hurt."

Bo brushed at his rear, disgusted at the amount of dust he sent flying. "And don't even get me started on the black horse." He turned a baleful eye toward the beautiful gelding, a look the horse returned. "He's a demon in horse clothing. He actually bucked me off. He didn't buck when anybody else got on him."

"I told you, Bo." Mr. Nelson sounded stern. "You can't crank his nose to his chest and then gig him in the sides. You told him to move but not to move forward. The only direction left was up. He did exactly what you told him to do."

On some level Bo understood what Mr. Nelson was telling him but the reality was the big black gelding had put him in the dirt at such speed he felt lucky he hadn't broken any bones.

"The appaloosa wouldn't even let me get my foot in the stirrup. I'd rather walk to Grayson, Dad. I really would." The tone of Bo's voice just missed whining.

Ed frowned. "We're one horse short for everybody to ride. I thought Flicker and Shelly could share since their combined weight would be easier on the horse than putting you two boys together."

He glanced at Mr. Nelson, exchanging some silent conversation that Bo could sense but not understand.

Ed gave a decisive nod. "Bo, you ride behind Flicker. She's a natural on the horses. All you'll have to do is sit and hang on."

Bo's mouth fell open. Shelly and Mark laughed.

Mr. Nelson showed them how to care for the horses before he left for home. Bo watched him leave, not envying him the mile-long walk home. Bo sighed and turned to look at the horses now milling in the corral. The saddles and bridles had been taken off but the horses wore halters.

Ed started barking orders. The children scattered. There was a lot to be done before morning.

Chapter 4

A loud rap on the door and a bellow woke them. "Boys, up and moving. We want to be on the road by sun-up."

Mark's feet hit the floor before Bo could pry his eyes open. In his eagerness to get to his parents, Mark had gone to bed with his clothes on so all he had to do was grab the small bag he'd packed the night before. He was out the door before Bo even sat up.

By the time Bo reached the kitchen the rest were milling around getting breakfast ready. He didn't like looking at his mother's face. Grace's eyes were red and puffy. Whenever she happened to look at Eden tears welled in her eyes and she would hastily wipe them away.

The little girl finally went to her mother and raised her arms up, demanding to be held. Grace broke. She pulled a chair away from the table and sat down, pulling the little girl onto her lap. Eden put her head on her mother's shoulder and waited for Grace to compose herself. The little girl was oddly calm.

"Don't cry, Mama. We'll be fine. Cosmos will find that old woman and Dalt won't hurt me. He's not a bad man."

"Oh, Ed." Grace looked at her husband. "I can't do this. I really can't."

Ed walked over to Grace and Eden. He crouched down until he was face-level with them. "Grace, do you want Mark to go alone?"

"Of course not." Grace shook her head in denial. "I don't want him to go at all. I know Claire would want him to stay here."

Ed sighed and reached out to stroke Eden's cheek before doing the same to Grace. "Honey, we both know Claire and Frank would have been here a week ago if they weren't in trouble. We need to send help."

He smiled, a slow, gentle, reassuring lightening of his face and eyes. "I can't think of any better help than Bo, Mark, Harley, and the girls. They know what's happened, and why. They've dealt before with the old woman and Dalt. Cosmos is out there and he'll keep an eye on them. And I believe the children can handle themselves in this situation."

Grace tightened her hold on Eden and whispered, "What about people? You know there are bad people out there. They'll be frightened and…" Grace's voice faltered. Her eyes widened from the horrible thoughts running through her head. "How do they protect themselves against frightened, panicked people?"

Ed turned to look at Harley.

The old man looked grimmer than Bo had ever seen him. He cleared his throat. "Grace, without going into a lot of details, believe me when I tell you I can take care of people. I learned how to protect myself early. I can keep us safe from thieves and worse."

Flicker, silent until now, spoke up. "Don't forget about me. I am a trained Hunter going into an area where I can make use of the magic that entered your world. Nobody untrained in the use of magic can stand against me. If the magic fails, I carry a nullifier. I have the means to protect us from evil-doers."

The young woman went to Grace and Eden. "I promise you the life I grew up in prepared me for situations like this. Your people have not lived in a world like mine. I have never known safety or peace. I have always had to protect myself from others. Look at me," she demanded.

She held her arms out. Even as small-boned and delicate as she appeared, she exuded an aura of competence and danger. Bo felt it from where he stood and watched his mother take courage from her words.

Flicker added, "I have been a Hunter for ten years— ever since I was twelve years old. I am alive and standing here before you because I'm very good at my job. I promise you if anything happens to your children it won't be from somebody hurting them."

Grace looked at Flicker, then down at Ed and Eden. She stroked her daughter's fly-away curls. Eden smiled at her with such sweetness and trust, Grace almost broke again. Her eyes went hard and stern as she looked at her youngest daughter.

She put her hands on Eden's face and leaned in until the little girl squirmed. "You listen to me, young lady. I need you to listen to Flicker. Learn from her. If we are going to have to live in this new world, I need you to be the very best you can be. Magic comes to you. I not only give you permission to use it, I *demand* you do so."

Eden looked rebellious, then resigned. "Yes, Mama. I'll try."

"Good." Grace put Eden down and stood up. "I'll have ration bags packed in a few minutes. By the time you have the horses saddled and bridled, I'll have them ready for you."

And those were the last words she spoke. She busied herself at the counter. Ed, Harley, Bo, Mark, and Eden went to the corral to saddle the horses. Flicker and Shelly stayed inside to help Grace.

***

Bo couldn't remember the last time he'd seen a saddle on Teddy. Eden most often rode him bareback. The little girl and the small pony were inseparable friends. Bo didn't worry about Eden staying in the saddle. The little girl had the agility of a monkey. He did wonder how the little pony would keep up with the big horses. An hour later, the sun shone with just enough strength to light up the road. Harley, riding the black gelding, took lead. Mark followed behind on the paint. Shelly's buckskin matched the paint, step for step. Eden, on Teddy, followed Mark and Shelly. Flicker, with Bo sitting behind her on the snowdrop appaloosa gelding, brought up the rear.

Teddy, competitive from head to hoof, held the pace. Bo hoped Eden didn't get tired of being bounced because the pony's jog looked rough to sit. Eden didn't look back.

Chapter 5

"Stop it." Flicker, with practiced ease, brought the appaloosa gelding under control. "Stop kicking him in the flanks. The horse will crow-hop, or bolt." She turned around in the saddle and glared at Bo. "Either of those actions will leave you in the dirt. Just how many bruises do you want?"

A few more inches backward would have sent him sliding off the horse's rump. Bo wiggled forward, getting as close to the saddle as he could. "Catch up with Uncle Harley. I want to talk to him."

Flicker sighed but obediently cued the horse to speed up. Bo grabbed for the back of the saddle and hung on.

As they passed the other horses Bo noticed Shelly and Mark had no trouble controlling their mounts. Teddy didn't like being passed by the bigger horse and Eden had her hands full pulling the pony back to a slower pace. A warm glow filled Bo when Eden won the battle. His little sister was a force to be reckoned with.

"Uncle Harley." Bo wiggled, trying to find a more comfortable position. The old man looked sharply at him before pulling back on his reins.

"Hop off, Bo. We'll take a break. You look like you want to talk and we'll talk easier in the shade of those trees. I could use a break from riding and so could the girls. We're all going to be sore from the unaccustomed exercise."

"You don't have to tell me twice." Bo swung his leg over the back of the horse and slid to the ground. The gelding stepped sideways. Flicker turned the horse toward the trees and kicked him into a trot. Mark, Eden, and Shelly followed her. Harley dismounted and, leading his horse, walked beside Bo.

"What's bothering you?" The old man sounded tired.

Bo wondered once again how much sleep his uncle had been getting. Only now did it occur to him that his father and uncle might have been keeping watch at night. Why hadn't he and Mark thought about that? "Like you said, we've been on the road for two hours. This is the main highway into Grayson. We haven't seen anybody. If people are leaving Grayson, evacuating like we've heard, shouldn't we see people walking? Or bicycling? It's…" Bo struggled to find words. "Not seeing anybody on the road is eerie."

Harley rubbed at his face, then smoothed his long beard. He took his hat off and wiped the sweat off his forehead. They reached the trees. Mark, Shelly, Flicker, and Eden had already dismounted. Shelly and Eden had their bags open, looking to see what their mother had packed for rations.

Harley glanced at the girls, clearly not wanting to worry them. "They're part of this," Bo reminded him. "We can't hide things from them. Not if we want to keep them safe."

Harley nodded. "You're right. Listen up, kids." Everyone stopped what they were doing, turning their attention to Harley.

"Walk around. Get the kinks out. Take the bridles off the horses and stake them like Mr. Nelson showed you.

We'll take a break now. Then we'll ride a few more hours and do the same thing. When we can't sit in the saddle any longer we'll camp for the night."

They busied themselves with the horses first. Only Flicker seemed genuinely comfortable with the process.

"You've done this a lot, haven't you?" Curiosity drove Bo to ask her.

She brushed the mane away from the appaloosa's neck, lifting it up and letting the breeze cool the sweat from the gelding's neck. "We don't have horses on our world but four-legged creatures that we ride in much the same way. Our world is more primitive than yours. We live in the magical realm, not a mechanized world." She gave a final pat to the horse, checking the stake to make sure it would secure the animal so he could graze. She turned back to Bo. "You'd do well to learn as much as you can because your world will, most likely, not remain mechanized. Magic and technology do not mesh well together."

Bo frowned at the horse, watching it drop its head, burying its nose in the deep grass. He sighed. "I know you're right, Flicker, but I can't say I'm happy about it."

She smiled in sympathy. "Walk around, Bo. You'll stiffen up if you don't. I'll go check on Eden."

"What's this?" Shelly, her small duffel bag spread open, pulled a ziplock bag out and held it up. Bo recognized the object a split second before Shelly did. She yelped, turned red, and stuffed the object back into her bag. Bo laughed.

Shelly grabbed the nearest object she could lay her hands on--a smooth round rock--and winged it at him. He caught it before it could hit him in the chest.

"I wonder if Mom sent a roll of toilet paper for all of us or if we're supposed to borrow yours?" Bo couldn't seem to stop laughing.

Mark unzipped his bag, laughing when he found his roll.

Uncle Harley gave a rusty chuckle. "You'll be glad you have that, little girl. Guard it well. In the coming days toilet paper will be more valuable than gold."

Mark pulled out a different pack. "This is welcome; enough jerky for way more than two days. It looks like she put in dried apples and peaches, too. The biggest problem I see is drinking water. We're lucky Missouri has natural springs but finding them might prove challenging."

The next fifteen minutes flew by with the children eating, walking, and disappearing into the bushes to relieve themselves. Flicker insisted the girls go in a group. No way would she allow Eden, or Shelly, out of her sight.

Bo returned to his original question. "Why aren't we seeing more people leaving Grayson? Have they evacuated already? Did the military send everybody a different direction? Will we even be able to find Uncle Frank and Aunt Claire?"

Mark, stretched out in the cool grass, sat up. He waited for Harley's response.

Harley pondered Bo's questions. "It's possible that whoever was leaving Grayson has already left. It's also possible the military are controlling evacuation routes. I don't think Frank and Claire would have gone somewhere else without getting word to Mark. I think the most likely answer has to do with your grandparents. I can't see Claire leaving without them. I think we'll get to Grayson and find out there is a logistics problem in moving them."

Mark looked hopeful and worried at the same time. "I didn't think about how difficult moving Grandma and Grandpa would be without a vehicle. I know Mom wouldn't leave without them. There must be a problem in getting them from Grayson to the farm."

Harley nodded. "I won't lie to you. Enough time has gone by since the sky ripped open that I think we need to be alert for panic. Fear creates danger. Don't trust anybody you see. If we do come up on people, don't be fooled. We stay in a group. We stay focused on our mission. Don't let yourself get sidetracked by anybody."

Flicker nodded in agreement, causing Bo to wonder about her life as a Hunter. Her life on a world more primitive than Earth must surely have given her a unique perspective on people.

Harley rose to his feet. "Back in the saddle. Break is over. Let's head out."

Refreshed and rested, the children managed to bridle their horses and mount. Bo had the hardest time since he had to get on behind Flicker. He ignored Mark's teasing and Shelly's smirk.

Once in place, he grinned down at Eden. "Lead us off, Edie." Then he forgot everything Flicker had told him and kicked the gelding in the flank. Amidst laughter, shouts, and bucking, Bo and Flicker took the lead.

Chapter 6

"Did you see the girl?" The old woman, Hemlock, glared at the big man standing before her. Her long, white hair lay in a sloppy braid down her back. On a good day, Dalt knew her eyes to be sea-green. On a day like today, angry at him, they had darkened until the green looked muddy and flat.

Dalt hung his head, not wanting to meet the old woman's eyes. He'd failed in his mission. *Watch the children. Isolate the little girl. Grab her and bring her to me.* Those had been his instructions. He'd not only failed, he'd lost the children.

"I'm sorry." Dalt struggled to think of a reason, an excuse for his failure. The children had been staying in an old house in the woods, cleaning the house and neatening the yard. In particular, Dalt had been fascinated by a metal machine the boys pushed around the yard to cut the long grass down. Dalt itched to get his hands on that machine.

He watched the children, but he gave a lot of thought to the strange tools used by the children. At night, he had touched the tools, tried them, careful to be quiet. But one night he'd fallen asleep, so deep and sound he didn't hear the children leave.

Dalt knew the rudiments of tracking. He'd seen Dragen do it often enough. Dalt thought Hemlock would be proud of him if he discovered where the children went. So he tried to find them and ended up lost, tired, and hungry. He risked a swift peek at Hemlock's face. Her green, gimlet-eyed gaze frightened him more than Dragen's mask ever had.

He rushed to speak, stumbling over his words in his haste. "I found their real house. Not the old one in the woods. I can find it again."

Hemlock made a sound of disgust. "Bah, I don't care about the house. I care about the girl and you say she's gone?"

Dalt, built like an ox, cowered before the old woman. In abject misery, he nodded. "Aye. I saw a man bring four-legged animals with seats strapped on them. This morning when I looked for the girl, everybody was gone. The animals were in the pen last night, and gone this morning. I didn't know which direction they went so I came to tell you."

Hemlock quivered with rage. "You're just now telling me this? The sun has been up for hours. They're riding and have a headstart on us?"

Dalt could have cried, he felt so bad about disappointing the old woman who had saved his life. When the sky ripped open, spilling them into this world, Dalt would have splattered on the ground if Hemlock hadn't performed a great feat of magic and saved him.

"I would have been here sooner but I didn't know how to find you without going back to the old house first. I had to backtrack my path."

Hemlock sighed, a sound she made often when dealing with Dalt. She needed his brute strength and complete obedience, leaving her no choice but to put up with his shortcomings.

"We have to be careful using magic." Hemlock pondered their situation. "We know the Executioner can track us if we misuse magic. But can he detect normal use of magic?"

Hemlock sank down onto her heels, thinking hard. Dalt followed suit.

"We know the air that came through the hole with us follows the little girl. She draws and holds it the same way a focus does on our world." The old woman stroked the big ugly rock she wore on her hand. Useless now. This world they fell into didn't respond to magic in any manner she was used to.

Her eyes lost focus as she searched the sky for magic. "There it is. Shining like a beacon. I can track that girl wherever she goes."

"Help me up, Dalt. Hemlock held her hand out to him. "Maybe it's better if the girl is away from her home. She'll have to go into the woods eventually. They have a big headstart on us thanks to your stupidity."

The mild calm in Dalt's eyes never changed. He rose to his feet and, with gentle hand, helped the old woman stand up.

Hemlock brushed his hands away, then stamped her feet on the ground to get the circulation going before stalking off through the woods. The road would have been faster, but she knew they were still being hunted by Cosmos. The last thing she'd do was make the hunt easy for him."

Chapter 7

"Pull up, kids." Harley reined in his horse. "We'll ride into the trees and find a safe place to camp. It's earlier than we planned on stopping but I think Eden's done for the day."

Bo hid a grin when he glanced at his youngest sister. She sat sideways in the saddle, Teddy's reins draped over the saddle horn. Only the pony's stubborn nature kept him following Harley's lead horse.

Bo's own rear had gone numb two hours ago. His legs were so numb he wasn't sure he'd be able to stand. Flicker, in front of him, seemed as fresh as when they'd left home. He envied her fit body and the lithe ease with which she rode the horse.

Only Mark looked like he'd protest, but then he looked down at his smallest cousin and saw her weary slump. He pulled his lips tight against whatever words he'd been about to say.

Shelly hadn't spoken a word in the last three hours. Bo knew his sister was riding on sheer willpower. Shelly took stubborn to limits even Teddy couldn't match.

Bo heard groans and moans in plenty as the small group dismounted and tended to the horses. But the sounds were good-natured and not complaining.

"One more day." Mark stroked the nose of the paint horse he'd ridden all day. The horse nickered and butted his chest. Mark slid his hand to the horse's neck, scratching and rubbing. He found an itchy spot. The horse stretched its neck out, and its lower lip quivered and shook until it resembled the floppy lower lip of a camel. Mark grinned. "Feels good, doesn't it?"

He gave the paint one final pat, a last scratch, and Mark felt ready to face the others. He didn't want to stop for the night, but knew he had no choice. But he'd get to Grayson by tomorrow night or leave the others in his dust.

"Gather around, children." Flicker knelt on the ground. With practiced ease she scraped away grass and rocks, clearing a small dish-shaped fire pit in the dirt. "This trip is a good opportunity for me to show you some advanced survival skills. Mark, you may already know some of this but I bet I have a few tips and tricks your father may not know about."

She smiled at Mark's grim face, trying to will the boy to smile back. He didn't, so she turned back to the fire pit and explained to them the mechanics of what type of wood worked best, and how to lay the kindling down first. She couldn't wait to show them how to create a small water cloud. It felt good to be doing a chore so familiar to her. She'd been so busy over the past few weeks, she hadn't realized how homesick she had been for her own world.

Holding her hands above the kindling, she wiggled her fingers and pictured the sparks that would set the wood on fire.

Nothing happened.

Flicker rocked back on her heels, looking thoughtful. She looked up, searching for the stream of magic that followed Eden around like a rainbow. Her thoughtful gaze turned to worry. She stood up but waved to the others. "Don't move. Stay right where you are."

With careful steps, keeping her eyes focused above, she began to walk backwards. "I can see the magic. The air sparkles with it. More than I've seen since I fell into your world, but it stops. It's like we're in a bubble."

She looked back at the children. "I want to try something. Shelly, I want you to stand here."

Flicker pointed to a spot in the clearing nearest the road. She circled the small clearing, placing the children at equal distance around the circumference. She left Harley in the center by the fire pit.

"Now," she said. "Let's see what it looks like." Again she looked upward, searching for the magic in the air. "I see it over Harley, over Bo, a lot of it swirling around Eden." Her eyes landed on Mark. She stopped talking. She almost stopped breathing.

"I see none of it around Mark." She stared at the boy. She waved a hand. "All of you, except Eden and Mark, come here and stand beside me."

Harley, Shelly, and Bo obeyed Flicker's instructions, leaving Eden on one side of the camp and Mark standing on the opposite side.

"What's happening?" Harley spoke in a low tone to Flicker. "You look worried."

Flicker gazed upward, looking at the magic swirling in the air. She pulled a black box off her tool belt, the same one she had used in the woods when Eden had been kidnapped by Hemlock and Dragen. She fiddled with the almost invisible buttons. When done, she returned the box to her belt. "I've sent out a call to Cosmos. He'll be here soon and we can talk about what this means."

She continued her explanation to Harley and the children. "When we entered your world, air from our world contaminated your atmosphere. Cosmos told us that your world would be changed. The unstable atoms that allow our minds to mold and create items by magic would set off a chain reaction on your world. Wherever the magic touches, it changes. What we didn't anticipate was the fact that your world doesn't accept magic in ways we are familiar with."

"Stay where you are," Flicker reminded Eden and Mark. "I need you to stand there for a short time. I'll explain why in a few minutes." She continued her explanation to the others.

"On our world we have never known a live person to hold magic. We can manipulate the air around us. We carry a focus where we store extra magic for those times and uses that require greater power than we have naturally." Flicker raised a hand to the amulet bag she wore around her neck. "I carry mine in this bag. It's just a rock, but I've discovered that it no longer holds magic. It doesn't work on this world."

"But Eden..." Flicker frowned and her eyes lost focus as she looked at the little girl. She didn't look at Eden but the air sparkling and swirling around the child, the magic air that followed Eden like a second skin. "She carries magic around her and through her."

Her eyes slid from Eden to Mark and her eyes darkened. "What we didn't anticipate, and have never seen, is a person who repels magic. There is a bubble around Mark where magic isn't."

Chapter 8

A bright beacon of light skimmed across the tree line. A moment later the black-clad figure of Cosmos descended to the ground. A creature of light, his shape was created by the clothing he wore.

A flat-brimmed black hat shadowed a head completely encased in sheer black cloth. The material molded to his face like a second skin.

He wore a long-sleeved black shirt cuffed tightly at the wrists. Black gloves made of the same form-fitting cloth that covered his face gave the impression they'd been painted onto his hands. His black pants would have been right at home on a swashbuckling pirate. He had them tucked into knee-high soft black leather boots. Swirling from shoulder to below the knees, he wore a coat resembling a duster worn by cowboys.

The only parts of Cosmos visible were his remarkable eyes. Looking into them one realized why he was called Cosmos. In his eyes, depending on his mood, one could see pieces of the universe.

He strode toward Flicker, tension and worry visible in he tightness of his shoulder and the length of his stride. "You wouldn't call me without reason." He halted, a low warning in his voice. "You do have a reason, don't you?"

Flicker flickered, her body going in and out of sight, until she gained enough control to stand her ground in the face of Cosmos's warning. "Of course I have a reason." In her anger she stalked toward him. "Look at Eden and tell me what you see."

Cosmos obediently looked at the little girl, his eyes a pure, serene blue with fluffy white clouds.

Flicker sounded grim as she said, "Now, look at Mark and tell me what you see."

Cosmos obediently turned his head to look at the tall youth. In his eyes, the white fluffy clouds floating in the blue blew from his eyes as if blown by gale-force winds. A burst of light beamed from his eyes before he dropped his lids to shut off the bright beacon.

Mark hit the ground, startled and trying to stay out of the light-burst from Cosmos's eyes. "What the heck was that? Are you trying to laser me?"

"Don't be silly." Cosmos sounded annoyed. "I'd never use something so primitive." He opened his eyes to reveal gray storm clouds in the left eye and an eagle's eye in the right. "Stay where you are. Don't move."

"Don't worry," Mark muttered. "I'm not budging."

"Stop." Cosmos held a hand up to stop Eden from running to Mark. "Do not move."

Eden looked scared but held her ground. Cosmos took his time, first examining her, then Mark. He pulled a box similar to the one Flicker carried in her tool belt out of a pocket hidden in the folds of his clothing and examined it closely.

Bo, curious, moved closer to watch. "Will we get one of those?"

Cosmos didn't take his eyes off the box. "All Hunters carry the tools of their trade, so, yes. When, and if, you complete your training you will receive one of these boxes. Not everything can be fixed by magic." He took his eyes off the box and turned to gaze into Bo's eyes. Bo, hard as it was to meet the eyes of Cosmos, held his ground. "You'd do well to remember that, Bo."

"Yes, sir." Relieved to be out from under Cosmos's eyes, Bo sidled over to stand by Harley and Shelly.

Cosmos turned back to Mark. "I want you to stand up and walk toward Eden. When I tell you to stop, you stop."

Mark got to his feet and nodded. "Yes, sir."

Cosmos's eyes lightened, sending the storm cloud away. Behind the dark cloth his lips turned upwards.

Mark started toward Eden and got to the middle of the clearing before Cosmos stopped him. Flicker stood at Cosmos's shoulder and they examined the two children and the air around them.

"Move toward Eden one step at a time," Cosmos instructed.

Mark nodded and started a slow step-by-step approach.

"Do you feel anything?" Cosmos asked.

Mark stopped and looked thoughtful. "Yeah, I do."

Eden nodded. "I do, too, Cos."

"Stand still, Mark. Eden, I want you to walk toward Mark."

The little girl started to run to her cousin but Cosmos stopped her. "No, no. One step at a time."

Eden nodded. Everybody smiled at her careful, baby steps, but Cosmos didn't correct her. The golden bird eye that had been in his right eye spread to both eyes as he watched the air surrounding the children.

"You can walk faster now, Eden." He told her.

She stopped and shook her head. "No, I can't. I'm trying, Cos, but it's hard."

"I was afraid of that," Cosmos said in a voice low enough to only be heard by Flicker. "We've got a problem on our hands. Thank you for calling me in. I needed to know about this."

"What's wrong?" Eden sounded scared. Her big blue eyes filled with tears. "I want Markie."

Mark ran toward the little girl, intending to scoop her into his arms to soothe her. When he got three feet from her, he ran into an invisible wall with enough force to send him reeling backward. Eden let out a yell and fell in the opposite direction.

Her wail of fear sent Shelly flying to her. Bo went to his cousin and gave him a hand up.

"What was that?" he asked Mark but he was looking at Flicker and Cosmos for the answer.

"That, my young friend," Cosmos said, looking as grim as his cloth-clad face could manage, "is a very big problem."

Chapter 9

A sober group gathered around the small fire pit. Mark sat farthest away, sitting a good five feet from the fire and double that from Eden. Nobody looked happy.

Eden huddled by Shelly, leaning against her side. Even in the dimming light as the sun went down, the dancing firelight could be seen in her blue eyes wet with tears. "I want to go sit with Markie."

Shelly hugged her little sister and looked helplessly at Cosmos. His eyes were so dark nothing could be seen in them. His voice, gentle and calm, answered Eden. "I'm sorry, little one. Until we figure out more about this condition its best if you stay farther apart." Cosmos went to her and knelt, bringing his face closer to hers. "Let's eat first. Flicker needs to access magic and if Mark sits too close, the magic doesn't work. Can you understand that?"

Eden stared into Cosmos's eyes, now swirling with purple and gold fog, then leaned in until her nose almost touched his cloth-covered one. "I'm five years old, not stupid." Then she drew back and buried her face against Shelly's shoulder.

A startled laugh burst from Cosmos before he stood up and glanced at Flicker. "That tells me. Show the children how to get water and fix us something to eat."

Flicker nodded. Cosmos strode off into the darkening woods.

Flicker put the children to work making food. Sticks became carrots, rocks were turned into potatoes. Some foods the children didn't recognize but Flicker assured them that on her world they were wonderfully delicious.

She delighted them when she showed them how to create a tiny raincloud over the soup pot. Each child took a turn at creating their own.

"The only hard part is getting it to hold steady in one place." Shelly, kneeling on the ground, looked up, her eyes shining with wonder and delight. Mark, watching from across the clearing, looked morose at her words.

Flicker taught as she cooked, trying to instill in them awareness of the rules of magic. "The number one rule." She looked at the children, the sternness in her wise eyes at odds on a face that looked younger than her years.

Bo, looking slightly bored, Shelly, over-achiever at all things academic, and Eden, obedient to Flicker's teachings spoke in unison: "What bleeds, breathes, and procreates, magic must not duplicate."

A smile, warm and big, lit up Flicker's face. "Perfect. Remember that and all the other rules become simple."

The children nodded. They understood hunting for meat far better than creating food from inanimate objects.

Mark, despite his determination to keep his distance, crept forward, earning a reprimand from Flicker. He returned to his designated seating area.

Bo took pity on him and went to sit next to him. "I guess you were right," he said as he plopped down beside his cousin. "When you told me you couldn't do magic. You can't feel it."

"I could at first." Mark frowned. "When we were at the old house getting it ready for Mom and Dad. When Shelly made the French fries. I felt it then. But instead of getting stronger, it faded away. Now, no matter how hard I try, I can't get it back."

Bo nodded. "Somehow you started insulating yourself against the tainted air. You created a bubble that you walk around in."

Mark looked miserable. He pulled his knees up and hugged them against his chest. "It felt better. More normal. I didn't realize what was happening to me."

His eyes grew damp and he wiped them away with his hand. "I didn't realize I was pushing Eden away. She hasn't hugged me in over two weeks. When I first came she was always crawling into my lap and kissing me on the cheek. Telling me she lov—" Mark's voice broke. He hid his head against his knees.

"I love that little girl," he mumbled. He raised his head and Bo saw such a look of anguish on his cousin's face he had to look away. "I can't bear the thought of never getting a hug from her again. I feel awful."

"Don't." Cosmos spoke behind them.

Mark and Bo let out yelps of alarm and fell over themselves rolling away. Both boys came boiling to their feet.

"Scare a guy, will you?" Bo, fists at the ready, glared where he thought Cosmos stood. The only way to see him in the darkness was the gleam—Bo suspected borrowed moonlight—glowing at eye-height.

"My gosh, warn a fellow when you're sneaking up behind him." Mark raised a shaky hand to brush hair from his eyes.

"I do apologize." The boys couldn't see Cosmos but they heard the laughter in his voice. "It's good to keep you on your toes."

Mark snorted. "I'm going to need a trip into the trees. You scared the p—"

Bo laughed and punched Mark in the arm to keep him from finishing the word. "The girls. Do you want Shelly lecturing you on what is proper for Eden to hear and what isn't?"

Mark fell silent but his glare spoke volumes. During this time of worry, Mark's sense of humor seemed to have taken a leave of absence.

With exquisite precision, Mark turned away from Bo to glare at Cosmos. "Did you have a reason for scaring the livers out of us?"

"I did, actually," Cosmos replied. "I want to run a few experiments. I'd like you to come with me."

"Now?" Mark looked surprised.

"Yes, now. There is a house a short walk from here. I looked around and it seems to be deserted. I'd like you to come with me for an hour or so."

Mark thought about his request, then shrugged his shoulders. "Sure, let's go."

"Bo." Cosmos stopped him. "I need you to stay with the girls. Dalt and Hemlock, if they aren't in the area, soon will be. They have to be aware that you children are no longer at home. Work with Flicker on self-defense skills while Mark and I are gone."

Bo hesitated, hating the conflict within him. He stepped back. "Yeah, Mom would kill me if anything happened to Shelly or Eden. I'll do what you say but don't be too long. I'll worry."

"Understood." Cosmos beckoned to Mark and the two vanished into the darkening night.

Chapter 10

"Are you sure nobody is here?" Mark whispered. "This feels wrong. We shouldn't break into somebody's house."

"The door was unlocked. I didn't break anything," Cosmos reminded him.

"But still, this is against the law." Mark, with every fiber of his being, wanted back in the clearing with his cousins.

"I'm a Hunter," Cosmos said. "I don't break the laws." He stopped and turned to stare at Mark, his eyes shrinking to pinpricks of light so sharp Mark looked away. "Magic changes the rules, Mark. I promise you we will do no harm."

They stood in the dark kitchen. Mark pulled a small flashlight from his pocket and turned it on. "At least the batteries still work."

"Explain to me, how does electricity work?" Cosmos asked.

Mark did his best to explain how the wires came to the house. His own knowledge was woefully lacking.

"This box with the fuses." Cosmos asked. "Where is it?"

"Usually in the basement," Mark said. "But you don't really want to see one, do you?"

"I do," Cosmos nodded. "Let's find this box."

"Oh, jeez," Mark groaned. "Nobody goes into a strange, dark basement in the dead of night."

"I'm a Hunter," Cosmos repeated. "I go where I need to go. If you don't like the dark then get behind me and stay out of my light."

Mark took two hasty steps backwards, flicking off his small flashlight and stuffing it back into his pocket. He'd seen what the light of Cosmos did to people and there was no way he'd risk it touching him. The light of Cosmos rendered judgment on the guilty. While Mark didn't feel like he'd committed any major crimes, he didn't want to become aware of things he might have done without full knowledge.

He positioned himself behind Cosmos, well away from the blinding white light pouring from Cosmos's eyes. Even the reflected light hurt his eyes, making them water. "Can you crank it down a notch?"

He felt Cosmos shake with laughter. "I'm sorry, youngling. I forget your human eyes are so sensitive."

"Yeah, yeah," Mark muttered. "Just find the basement and let's get out of here."

With Cosmos lighting the way it didn't take long to find the stairs leading downward.

Mark directed Cosmos. "The box is usually on the wall closest to the power poles."

"That wall, then." Cosmos pointed and the two started a slow walk toward it.

"What are you hoping for?" Mark asked. "There has to be a reason why you brought me here."

"There is." Cosmos spoke absently. "And I think we're just about there."

Mark heard a snap; a few more steps and the air seemed to crackle. One more step and the little sharp sound became an audible hum. Three feet from the breaker box, Cosmos's eyes went dark just as every light in the house went on.

Mark froze. "Whoa, what happened? What did you do?"

"I, my young friend, did nothing." Cosmos turned around, his eyes sparkling as if lit by a thousand fireflies. "Where you are, magic isn't. I wanted to see if getting you close enough to a power source would allow the power to function normally."

Mark shook his head. "But the lines coming into the house are surrounded by contaminated air. Why would standing by the box make any difference?"

"I don't pretend to understand anything on a mechanized world but I think everything is working fine. Nothing is broken. The electricity is still here. Magic nullifies its effects. You nullify magic, thus allowing it to work normally. The wires must carry your repulsion along the lines. I wish I could see everything along the lines outside the house to see if this follows the wires to every house, or if it's just here in this one."

Mark shook his head. "None of this makes sense to me. How can electricity be generated if the power plant isn't running? Is it stored like batteries?"

Cosmos shook his head. "I don't know. I think if there are more people like you who can nullify the effects of magic, your world might be able to continue using technology. I've never known a world to be both magical and mechanized." His eyes went dark and stormy, intermittent lightning flashes flickering in their depths. "You're going to be in very high demand by others once this is known."

Mark felt his stomach tighten, suspicion turned to alarm. "What if there aren't others like me?"

Lightning flashed one last time to be replaced by swirling fog and shadows. Cosmos went utterly and completely still. His voice dropped to a low whisper. "If that happens, Mark, you must never let anybody know what you can do. There are powers out there that would fight a war to possess your ability. Now, be very quiet and move away from the box."

A door slammed upstairs. Mark heard excited voices. "Lights. Oh, man, the power is on."

He heard men's voices. At least three, from what Mark could discern.

Cosmos grabbed Mark's sleeve and pulled him across the basement floor toward the bottom of the stairs leading up. Five feet from the breaker box the house went dark. The voices upstairs let out loud angry yells followed by crashes as they bumped into furniture in the dark.

Mark, afraid of being overheard by the men upstairs, kept his voice low. "Darn it, Cos. We shouldn't be in somebody else's house. Those men are going to cause a lot of damage."

"Whether we are here or not, those men would be. I needed to know if your ability to nullify magic would affect electricity. This was the closest house without going back to the farm."

In the dark of the basement Cosmos was all but invisible. Mark knew where the man was only by feel. Crashes and cursing continued upstairs. His hair stood on end when he heard someone say, "The lights were just on. Maybe the breaker box needs reset."

"Crap," Mark hissed. "They're going to come down here."

He felt Cosmos move. The long black coat Cosmos wore was put into his hands. Cosmos shoved him hard against the wall. "Get down. Cover yourself and don't move. Don't peek, unless you feel like facing judgment today."

"Not particularly." Mark tightened his hold on the coat. Cosmos didn't have to tell him twice. He sank down to the floor and curled into a tight ball, pulling the coat over the top of him. In the dark, he felt confident nobody would see him. He listened to the progress of the men as they stumbled and cursed their way to the stairs leading to the basement.

Mark pulled himself into a tighter ball. What was Cosmos waiting for?

He could hear anger in the voices of the men. Had they all come down or did someone stay upstairs?

He could distinguish the voices now. Two voices, not three. Someone had stayed upstairs.

"We need light," the higher voice said. "If you have any of those matches left, now would be a good time to use one."

They were beside him now, close enough that Mark heard the striking of a match. With luck, maybe they would walk right past Cosmos. He'd be very hard to see if he stayed in the shadows.

Luck seemed to favor them as the men moved toward the far wall, but a deeper voice cursed as his match burned low. "I'll light another one," deep-voice said.

Mark heard the scraping of another match being lit. Then a startled, "What the h--?" Then the screaming started.

Under the coat, Mark huddled and tried to close out the sounds by holding his hands over his ears, but he heard the sounds anyway.

Above the screams, Mark listened to footsteps running across the floorboards above them. A door slammed and he knew the third man fled. He couldn't blame him. If he had a choice, he'd run too, but coming out from under the coat would expose him to the Light of Truth. There was no way he'd risk that horror. He'd seen Eden go through the judgment and he knew the little girl still suffered from nightmares.

"Almost done," Cosmos said. "Stay covered. Do not emerge until I give you an all clear."

"No problem," Mark muttered. "I'm not poking my nose out until you tell me to."

An undetermined amount of time passed. Mark heard sounds and smelled odors he didn't ever want explained.

"All clear." Cosmos lifted the black coat off and put it back on. Soft moonlight glowed in his eyes, giving just enough light to see by.

Mark, stiff from sitting huddled so long, took his time standing up. He peered carefully around the basement. "Where are they? I don't want to step on anybody."

Cosmos gripped his arm and pulled him toward the stairs. The moonlight pouring from his eyes lit the darkness with a soft, warm glow. "There is nothing left to step on. Those were very bad men. I thought they were frightened townspeople fleeing from Grayson. Frightened people are usually good people. These men were something else. The light revealed these were evil men who had been locked up. When the electricity stopped working, many of these men escaped. I am very glad I was able to render judgment."

They stood at the kitchen door now, ready to go outside. Mark halted, horror filling him. "You mean those men were escaped convicts? The countryside is full of roaming criminals?"

Cosmos sounded impatient. "I know these were bad men. Men who murder the innocent. I rendered judgment. They did not survive. When the family who lives here returns, they will never know what happened here. I cleaned up the mess."

Mark's stomach tipped. "Cleaned up the mess? What does that mean? You didn't eat them, did you?"

"What?" Cosmos sounded so horrified that Mark felt instant relief.

"I want to know how you cleaned them up. Where did the bodies go? You didn't have much time in there." Mark pushed, driven by the need to know how one minute two men stood in judgment, alive and evil, and then nothing, not even blood, marking where they had stood. "What did you do?"

Cosmos sighed, a remarkably human sound to be made by a being composed of light. "We really don't have time to be talking about this. Now that I know your world has such evil in it I need to get back to the clearing and help Flicker keep the others safe. It's not just Hemlock and Dalt we need to worry about anymore."

"Just tell me," Mark insisted. "I need to know."

Cosmos opened the door and pulled Mark out into the night air. "On the magical worlds we don't bury our dead like you seem to do here. We use purification. Just as we have Hunters and Teachers, we also have Purifiers, whose job is to purify the land."

Cosmos continued before Mark could ask what this meant. "Purification is a disintegration of the body. We cleanse by holy fire. Holy fire doesn't burn anything but the body and when we are done, nothing of the body remains. It is gone and the area where it lay is purified and clean. It keeps the land clean and the air free of disease."

Cosmos halted, forcing Mark to stop walking. "Believe me, Mark. If anybody needed purifying, those two men did. They spent most of their lives doing evil. When I searched for their souls, the place where I should have found them had been empty for years. Those men were empty vessels. I have never known a soulless vessel that could be saved."

Mark, mulling over Cosmos's words, couldn't think of anything else to ask. "I heard the third man leave the house. He's out here somewhere."

Cosmos nodded. "Yes, I know. We must get back to the clearing. Once I know everybody is warned and safe, I will go hunt for him. The people on your world do not yet know about Hunters. I should be able to find him if he's still in the area."

"Okay," Mark agreed. "Let's get back to the clearing." He fell silent.

Cosmos brightened the light coming from his eyes and they ran through the night.

Chapter 11

Cosmos grabbed Mark's arm as they approached the clearing. "Wait, Mark. Make sure Flicker hasn't created some nasty surprises for the unwary."

Mark stopped and waited. Cosmos looked down at him with eyes that somehow managed to convey curiosity.

"Tell me, Mark. Do you feel anything strange?"

Mark snorted. "Don't even get me started on strange. Ever since the sky ripped open and we found there are other worlds my life has been nothing but strange. What do you want from me?"

"I want you to walk into the clearing." Cosmos pushed him gently.

Suspicious but obedient, Mark pushed through the bushes and shrubs hiding the clearing from the road. Nothing happened. He turned to tell Cosmos. Nobody stood behind him. He backtracked and poked his head through the bushes. "Aren't you coming?"

"I would, Mark." Cosmos cocked his head. "I can't. Not until Flicker turns off her safeguards."

"What would happen to you?" Mark returned to Cosmos's side.

"Nothing pleasant." Cosmos's eyes turned dark and fiery.

"Where I am, magic isn't." Mark felt a grim foreboding. The ramifications of his ability still hadn't completely sunk in yet. "Can you go in with me?"

"In the basement, you had to be within several strides of the breaker box before it worked." Cosmos sounded thoughtful. "I have no idea if your ability to nullify magic extends beyond yourself. Electricity worked in a normal manner when you were close enough. Let's see if I can enter with you. This is information we need to gather."

He placed a hand on Mark's shoulder and, Mark leading the way, they pushed through the bushes into the clearing.

"I felt nothing." Cosmos spoke softly into Mark's ear. He squeezed Mark's shoulder and stepped away. "This is disturbing on many levels. It shows me that Eden being a human focus is just the beginning of the problems we're going to face. Magic is mutating on your Earth in ways we've never seen. I very much fear our Teachers are going to be learning as much as they teach."

Noisy greetings drowned out further conversation between Mark and Cosmos.

Flicker, Hunter by inclination and by training, frowned at Cosmos. "If Mark can walk right through our protections, does that mean others can too?"

Cosmos shook his head. "We don't have enough information. To my knowledge, Mark is the only being I've ever known who can repel magic. Until we know otherwise we should assume there are others like him. Our safety lies in expecting the worst."

Flicker's frown deepened. Eden looked scared. Harley ruffled the little girl's hair. "Buck up, Edie. We're safe enough with Flicker and Cosmos. Silas will return soon with more help."

Shelly smiled at her uncle and hugged her little sister. "That's right, Edie. Don't be scared."

Harley handed Shelly his mug of water. "Could you turn this into coffee for me, Shelly?"

"Sure." Shelly took the cup, frowned at Mark and moved a careful distance away from him. It took her longer than it should have but she soon had a mug of hot, steaming coffee. She handed it back to Harley, who smiled his thanks.

Mark felt a pang of regret. Magic would never come to him and he'd do well not to wish for the experience.

He sank down by the fire and tuned out Cosmos. He didn't need to relive their adventure. He'd lived it. Their voices faded into background noise. Mark turned his thoughts to tomorrow. He needed to know if his parents were alive and well. Nothing else mattered to him right now.

"If Mark nullifies the effects of magic, and we can't trust the safeguards I put in place, how do we maintain camp safety?" Flicker's voice, agitated and shrill, brought Mark back to the present and away from his memories of Grayson.

"We're all tired," Cosmos soothed. "We'll put Mark in the middle. For right now, his bubble of magic-free air is small. To get to him, an intruder would have to move through twenty feet of protected space."

"What if I need to go relieve myself?" Mark asked. "Every time I walk out of the clearing I leave a potential hole for others to enter through."

Harley, gruff and matter of fact, said, "Go right before we sleep for the night. Flicker and Cosmos will make sure all the protections are in place once you're back."

"Actually," Cosmos added, "go in groups. The girls go with Flicker. I'll take the men. That way we'll be able to protect each other from potential harm."

Nobody was happy with that idea, but everybody was tired. Before long, bedrolls were out. Mark found himself alone by the dying embers of the fire. He couldn't blame the others for not wanting to be too near. Heck, he didn't like the idea of sleeping in unprotected air. Hemlock and Dalt continued to be a very real threat.

Cosmos stayed until everybody settled and slept. Then he walked to the far edge of the clearing and used his nullifier to open a small hole. Just as carefully he closed the protective circle before lifting skyward. Let the hunt begin.

Chapter 12

"Cosmos will return when he finishes what he's doing." Flicker spoke impatiently. "Right now, we need to concentrate on getting Mark's family out of Grayson. I don't know how we're going to do that if we can't get in." She sent a baleful look down the road to where barricades blocked the road into Grayson.

The paint horse, sensing Mark's agitation, side-stepped, tossing his head and pulling on the bit. Mark tightened his grip on the reins. "What would happen if I just kick him in the sides and race through the road-block?" he demanded.

"They'd shoot you, your horse, and most likely the rest of us." Harley's voice cracked with the force of a whip lash. "Settle down, boy. We need to think, not go off half-cocked. It never occurred to any of us that Grayson would be under quarantine. Nobody going in. Nobody allowed out. They must be afraid the people living here will carry the contamination. They don't realize yet that it's not spread by people but by the very air they breathe."

"They realize." Bo leaned to the side to peer around Flicker at the armed guards manning the barrier. "They're wearing face masks."

"Will they talk to us? Flicker asked.

Harley shook his head. "No, they already told us to go back where we came from. When I asked them if they could give me information about Mark's parents, one of them pointed his weapon at me and told me to take the boy away and forget he ever had parents."

"That doesn't sound right," Shelly burst out. "It's our family. We have a right to know."

"Let's go." Harley spoke abruptly. "They're sending two armed guards our way. We don't want to risk them confiscating the horses. I would if I was in charge."

They turned the horses around and cantered away from Grayson. Harley kept them moving until a curve in the road hid them from sight. "There." He pointed to the right. "Push through the brush there and keep going until we're far enough from the road not to be seen."

Nobody spoke, the only noise the creaking of leather and jangling of bits as they rode deeper into the woods.

"Dismount," Harley ordered. Once on the ground he continued. "Take care of the horses but leave them ready to ride for a little while. Flicker, set up whatever safeguards you can manage. We don't want any military patrols to find us."

"Isn't that a kick?" Bo murmured to Mark. "We've gone from worrying about an old woman and a big, stupid man to being afraid of our own soldiers. They should be the ones we turn to, not hide from."

Mark nodded. So close to home and yet so far. He leaned closer to Bo and spoke softly, not wanting to be overheard. "I'm going to slip away and get to the house. I know a way that only a kid would know about."

Bo gave his cousin a long, measuring look. "Are you sure you can get there without being shot?"

Mark nodded.

Bo opened his mouth and yelled, "Uncle Harley, Mark has a plan." Then he yelped again when Mark punched him in the arm.

"You jerk." Mark punched Bo again for good measure. "If I wanted everybody to know I'd have told them myself."

"I'm not a jerk." Bo rubbed his arm. "I'm a team player. We're on a mission as a group. Not each of us going off in different directions. We need to know what you're planning, how you're going to accomplish your goal, and..." He glared at Mark. "We need a rescue plan in place if you fail."

"All right," Mark said. "But warn a fellow next time. I won't tell you any secrets if you're going to blab them the minute I get the idea out of my mouth."

"Blab away." Bo waved his hand. "We're all ears."

They waited for Flicker to finish securing the campsite. Eden trailed at her side, watching and listening.

"What's your plan, Mark?" Harley's blue eyes, even at age 67, were shrewd and clear. The old man had left home at 14 and life hadn't been kind. He'd lived a life that left him seasoned and tough.

"I know a way into Grayson only kids use. You have to belly-crawl through some dense underbrush. You come out by the privacy fencing that runs along the back of my parents' subdivision. Old man Petersen never keeps his fence in good repair. We slip through his fence all the time. The only thing we'll need to worry about is Petersen's dog. He's mean and he bites."

Harley looked thoughtful. "You're sure this pathway won't be known about and guarded?"

Mark shook his head. "None of us kids who used it would tell a grown-up about the hidden pathway. Especially now the town is locked down. We'd want to keep an escape route open."

"What do you think?" Harley looked at Flicker.

The young woman gave the plan serious thought. She looked at the boys, a long, measuring perusal. "I think, at some point, we're going to have to trust them to be inventive and independent. I'm not kidding," she added. "In the magical realms these two would already be Hunters. Even at their young age, they would be through basic training and paired with an experienced Hunter to complete their training."

She narrowed her eyes, holding the boys' attention long enough for them to realize the seriousness of her next words. "I say we let Mark carry out his plan. Bo can go with him for backup. I want you back by sundown or I'll call Cosmos in to find you and you won't like it if he's pulled away from his mission. He has other ways of inflicting discipline than using the Light of Truth."

The boys nodded. Neither of them wanted to be on the wrong side of the Executioner.

"I understand," Mark assured her.

"Then go." Flicker nodded at him. "Find out what's happened to your parents and report back here by sundown."

Harley grabbed Mark by the shoulder. "Wait a minute. I have something for you."

He went back to the black gelding and pulled off the duffel bag tied behind the saddle. Unzipping a side pocket, he reached in and pulled out several items.

Mark recognized them. "You kept Ian's weapons, didn't you?"

Harley spoke, his voice gruff with emotion. "Ian didn't need them returned. Not where he was going. I figured there might come a time when we could use them. Take your pick."

Bo and Mark looked over the weapons. Bo chose a slim, wicked-looking dagger in a wrist scabbard and a well-used slingshot. He stuck the slingshot in his back pocket and tied the leather bag holding nicely rounded stones to a belt loop.

Mark chose a bigger knife, old and well-honed in a sheath that he strapped to his thigh. It felt odd to carry a weapon but also strangely right.

"Thank you, Uncle Harley. I'm glad you thought ahead. I do feel better having a weapon."

Flicker came up to them. She held out a small leather pouch. "On our world we rely on magic. Maybe too much. But we also have tricks. Use this on the fierce dog if you need to. It won't hurt him but may give him something else to think about than eating you."

She hugged them hard. "I don't like splitting our group up but we need information. Get in. Get the information we need. Then get back here." She went back to caring for the horses.

Shelly scowled. "Why can't I go with the boys? I can help them."

Flicker eyed the girl with sympathy and shook her head. "I'm sorry, Shelly. Eden needs you. With the boys gone I need you to help protect the campsite. Harley is well-versed in physical combat but Hemlock and Dalt will use magic. Of you all, I see you as the one showing the most promise. Eden is gifted, but she's afraid to use her power. She's too young. You show a true understanding of what magic is and how to use it. I need you here."

Bo could tell Shelly didn't like what Flicker said but she nodded and dropped the subject. Eden raised her arms to Bo. He lifted her up. She wrapped her arms around his neck and hugged him tight. Seeing her cry brought an answering moisture to his eyes but he blinked hard and the tears dried before they fell. He lowered Eden to the ground.

Eden looked at Mark, her mouth hardening into a stubborn look that usually struck terror to Bo's heart. This time the look was directed at Mark. Bo stepped back next to Shelly and they watched with interest to see what their little sister would do next.

She stepped toward Mark, an unseen breeze lifting her hair and swirling it around her head in a wild abandon. She stopped, her hands clenching into tight fists on her hips. "Mark, stop it. I need to hug you."

Mark clenched his jaw. Bo bumped Shelly with his elbow and leaned down to whisper in her ear. "Who knew Mark and Eden looked so much alike?"

She grinned. "Yeah, they have the same mouth."

"Stubborn." They spoke in unison, grinned, and turned back to watch.

They could see Mark take a couple of deep, deliberate breaths. He rolled his head, shook his shoulders, and looked grimly determined. The hair blowing around Eden's head calmed down. She ran to Mark and he picked her up, just as Bo had done a few minutes earlier.

Eden squeezed him tight before pulling away from him and sending him a bright, blinding smile.

"Thank you, Edie. I needed that hug."

Her blue eyes glistened, "I know you did, Markie. That's why I did it." She hugged him again then wiggled to be put down.

Bo straightened up and moved away from Shelly. He pointed in the direction of Grayson. "Let's go, Mark. Lead off."

Marked nodded. They said their goodbyes before slipping away through the underbrush, working their way toward Mark's home.

Chapter 13

"The board's still loose," Mark whispered. "Old man Petersen hasn't fixed it yet." He shifted the board to one side and pushed the one beside it the other direction, opening a gap big enough for a boy to crawl through.

"Hurry up," Mark urged Bo. "I don't want Petersen's dog to see us."

Bo wiggled and scooted through the opening. He stood up while Mark fixed the boards so they looked normal.

The slamming of a screen door froze the boys. "Run," Mark hissed. The sound of a dog barking lent wings to their feet.

The dog beat them to the fence and stood between them and freedom.

"That's the mean dog?" Bo panted in Mark's ear. "It's a Chihuahua. He probably doesn't weigh four pounds."

Mark turned to glare at Bo. "Don't underestimate him. He's an ankle biter. All the kids in the neighborhood carry his teeth marks."

Bo stood there, looking down at the tiny creature defending his territory. The little dog yapped and quivered, fierce little growls erupting from behind bared teeth. Nobody was getting through the gate on his watch.

Mark reached down to the knife strapped to his leg.

"You're not really going to hurt that little fella, are you?" Bo protested.

Mark's lips curled in a snarl. Bo hid a grin, knowing his cousin wouldn't appreciate having his resemblance to the little dog pointed out.

"I'm going home, Bo. All I have to do is get through that gate. No little yapper is going to stop me."

Bo could tell Mark meant what he said. He pulled the leather pouch out of his pocket, opened it up, and threw a handful of granules at the dog. He had no idea what the powder would do but he trusted Flicker. If she said this would work on the dog, he'd give it a try.

Rainbow colors, sparkling like glitter, sprinkled the dog. He growled, snapped at the sprinkles, then froze. His eyes glazed over. He looked past the boys and seemed to see something behind them. So intent and focused was his gaze that both boys turned to see what the little dog was looking at. A happy yip burst from the Chihuahua. He bolted for the middle of the yard.

"Do you see anything?" Bo frowned.

Mark shook his head. "Never mind. Let's go while the going is good."

He opened the gate and they slipped through.

"Home," Mark choked out, then broke into a run, stopping at the kitchen door. He turned the handle. "Locked." He sounded stupefied. "Mom never locks the back door. I hope they're here. Wouldn't it be awful if I came home and they're gone? Where would I even know to look?"

"Don't panic," Bo said. "Calm down and knock on the door."

He could have held his words because Mark was already pounding. Footsteps sounded. Bo saw the curtain in the kitchen window twitch. Even with the house closed tight, they heard a startled shriek.

"I'd know Aunt Claire's scream anywhere," Bo drawled and stepped away from the door. None too soon, the door banged open.

Bo's Uncle Frank pulled the boys into the house. Words were useless for the next few minutes. Bo tried, but couldn't escape being hugged and kissed by his aunt and uncle.

Aunt Claire pulled them toward the kitchen. "I don't have much to offer you. We're out of almost everything. But I can fix you tea."

Bo wanted to protest, to tell her they didn't require anything but he realized she needed to take care of them so he stayed silent.

Mark looked a lot like his father. Frank was tall and lean, his brown hair slightly thinning in front; his brown eyes shone brightly behind sturdy black glasses.

Aunt Claire was Bo's dad's sister. She had his blue eyes, the same blue as Eden's. Claire's blond hair had faded a bit with age. He didn't remember her having any gray in her hair but maybe he just hadn't noticed. Their smiles warmed him to his toes.

"I hoped somebody would come, but I never dreamed it would be you. How did you manage to get past the road-block?" Uncle Frank pulled Mark into another bear hug and clapped Bo so hard on the shoulder his knees almost buckled. "I need as much information as you can give me." He abruptly changed the subject. "Where's Harley?"

"With the girls," Mark replied. "He's fine. I knew a back way here. He stayed to help keep the girls safe."

Bo and Mark, each tripping over the other's words, told them about Dragen and the renegades how Hemlock and Dalt were still at large and why Eden had become a target.

They tried to explain about magic, but with Mark sitting so close, Bo's own grasp of magic wasn't strong enough to display any.

"Eden is a focus," Mark explained. "She's a magnet for magic, but I nullify it. Flicker will explain it to you when you meet her. When can you go? We need to get you out of here as soon as possible."

Frank started to speak, but Claire stopped him with a head shake. She wiped the tears from her cheeks. "No, Frank. I'll explain." She turned to the boys. "We started to leave a week ago. The roadblocks weren't in place yet. The military was encouraging people to leave, wanting the town evacuated. Then, suddenly, they changed their minds and shut down all the routes leaving town. We went from being forced to leave our homes to being prisoners in our own town."

Claire choked and began to cry again. "We should have left. We would have, except I couldn't leave Mom in the nursing home. I just can't."

Frank sighed and pulled his wife into a hug. He stood there, holding her while she wept.

Mark looked miserable. "What about Grandpa? Is he still alive?"

Frank nodded. "Yes, your grandmother is vague and forgetful, but she's physically healthy. We could have gotten her out with us but it didn't seem right to take her away from your grandfather. He's the one person she still seems to feel connected to. Your mom felt that taking May and leaving John would be cruel to both of them. Then we grew concerned about the level of care they're getting at the nursing home."

Claire raised her head off Frank's shoulder. Mark handed her a dishtowel. She gave him a watery smile and scrubbed her face dry. "Thank you, Mark." She pulled a chair out and sat down at the table.

Frank continued. "Food is scarce. Medical help is getting siphoned away from the nursing home. Nobody knows where they are being relocated to. People are scared. I'd feel better if you boys went back to the farm and waited for us. We'll get out eventually."

Bo could hear the warning in Frank's voice. The grim set to his lips and in his eyes tightened Bo's stomach in to a hard knot. "What are you trying not to tell us, Uncle Frank?"

Frank sighed and pulled the chair next to Claire out. He sat down across the table from Mark and Bo.

"Claire and I go to visit the folks every day. We make sure they are still being cared for, but the level of care is deteriorating. We've put in a request to bring them home. Our request has been approved. We intend to bring them here tomorrow."

"That's good." Bo nodded. "If you're all together, we can figure out a way to get everybody out of town."

"You don't understand," Frank said. "John is unable to walk, talk, or feed himself. May is physically fine but she won't know any of us. In a way, she's more difficult to handle than John is. She's like a flighty bird." His voice trailed off.

Mark leaned toward his father. "You don't know the resources we have. Flicker can use magic. Eden is really good if she'd get over being worried about using it wrong and making a mistake. Shelly is learning. We can make food, and water. Well, *they* can." He sank back in his chair.

Bo took over. "We have horses. If we can get hold of a wagon we can carry Grandpa and Grandma. We won't have to carry them. Grandma wouldn't have to walk if she didn't want to. Surely somebody in the area has a horse-drawn wagon."

Frank looked thoughtful. "I think Ben Higgins has an old wagon at his place. It might need some repairs made. Is that something your 'magic' might be able to fix?"

Mark nodded. "If Flicker can turn a stick into a carrot, she can fix a wagon. I know she can."

Claire shook her head at the idea of eating sticks. Bo had felt the same until he'd seen it done. Aunt Claire and Uncle Frank would learn fast enough what magic could do.

Frank frowned, looking thoughtful. "I'll go back with you. We won't have any inspections on the house for a few days. We just went through one. I'll see what your resources are. Talk to Harley. If you've got horses we can ride over to Higgins's farm and see if he has a wagon and what it would take to make it usable."

"Claire?" Frank reached over and covered her hand with his. "Tomorrow, we'll get your parents out of the nursing home. Once they are in our care, we'll figure out how to get out of Grayson and get back to the homestead. While I'm gone, you get things ready."

She nodded. Frank stood up and leaned over to kiss her on the cheek. "I'll be back by nightfall."

Mark and Bo stood up. Claire hugged Mark tightly. Despite Bo's protests, she pulled him into a hug too.

Mark opened the back door. "All we have to do is get past Petersen's dog."

Chapter 14

"What's wrong with Mr. Petersen's dog?" Frank asked the boys.

They glanced at the little dog jumping and spinning in the middle of the yard.

"Bo sprinkled him with happy dust," Mark said.

Bo shrugged. Calling the bag of powder 'happy dust' worked for him. He'd definitely remember to ask Flicker how to make it. He knew a few bullies that could use a dose.

The hole in the fence was a challenge for Frank, who was taller and broader than either of the boys. He took one look at the narrow opening, then backed up a few steps, ran for the fence, grabbed the top, and hauled himself over. He did it with such speed and confidence Bo doubted anybody had time to notice.

They belly-crawled through the brush following the pathway of countless boys. Bo would have enjoyed himself if the situation had been less dire. Twenty minutes later they halted at a tree with a red ribbon tied to a low-hanging branch, Shelly's warning that safeguards were in place past this point.

Mark stuck his fingers in his mouth and let loose a sharp whistle. A few minutes later Shelly popped up from behind a bush and waved them in.

"Flicker dropped the guards. She'll put them back

in place as soon as you're inside the clearing. She wants Mark in the middle of the clearing as fast as he can get there. She can't be sure of the protections until she knows he's not going to nullify any of it."

Mark nodded and took off, moving faster than the others. Frank, not wanting to let his son out of his sight, jogged after him.

On entering the clearing, Frank went straight to Harley and grabbed the old man in a bear hug. "Thank you for keeping Mark safe. Is what the boys told me true?"

"True as can be." Harley nodded.

Eden and Shelly ran to their Uncle Frank. He swung Eden up in his arms and the little girl buried her face in his shoulder. Shelly beamed at him with a happy smile, relief evident in her eyes. Uncle Frank wasn't her daddy, but he came in a close second.

Frank set Eden down. Shelly grabbed his hand and pulled him toward Flicker.

Eden grabbed his other hand. "Come meet Flicker, Uncle Frank. She's my teacher."

Shelly shook her head and tugged harder. "Not really a teacher. She's a Hunter. She's teaching us about magic until Silas gets back."

"Silas can fly, Uncle Frank." Eden's eyes sparkled. "When he flies, you can almost see wings on him but when he's on the ground you don't see anything. Isn't that amazing, Uncle Frank?"

Flicker looked like a shy bird standing in front of the tall man. She didn't actually flick but her body blurred around the edges a bit until she literally pulled herself back together.

"It's a pleasure to meet you." She tipped her head while maintaining eye contact with him. "My job is to train the boys to be hunters until such time as they can be apprenticed. I am to teach the girls how to use magic in an appropriate manner. But my prime directive is to keep Eden safe from harm. Hemlock would very much like to get hold of Eden. We must never let that happen."

Mark sat down next to his father. "Cosmos is hunting for Hemlock and Dalt. I'd try to describe Cosmos to you but you won't understand until you meet him. Silas took Dragen and Ian back to their world to begin their punishment. He'll find us when he gets back."

Mark's eyes turned somber, and he looked older than his thirteen years. "Our way of life is changing and there is no way to stop it. We're all going to have to learn how to adapt or die"

Frank nodded at Shelly when she handed him a jug of hot liquid. "I already know that. We haven't been able to access anything that uses electricity. The phones aren't working. The National Guard moved into the town within forty eight hours of what we thought was simply a strange weather phenomenon. They haven't left and their attitude has been changing. They started off being helpful and protective, but now they're treating us like prisoners. I'm beginning to be afraid they will start shooting at anything that moves."

He took a sip from his mug and smiled in pure bliss. "Where did you get the coffee? We've been out for days."

Shelly smiled. "I made it, Uncle Frank. I hope it's good. I only tasted coffee once and I tried to remember. Did I get it right?"

"It's wonderful. No bitterness." He took another swallow, slower this time, rolling the liquid around on his tongue. "In fact, if I didn't know better, I'd think there was vanilla or hazelnut of some flavor in here that I don't normally taste in coffee."

She giggled. "That might be because I tasted Mom's coffee from Starbucks. It was hazelnut crème. I don't know what regular coffee tastes like."

Frank smiled back at his niece. "It's good. I don't know where you got Starbucks coffee out here but I appreciate you sharing it."

The children laughed. They knew where Shelly had gotten the coffee from, but Frank still didn't understand. Even though they had told him about magic, it hadn't sunk in yet.

Flicker looked thoughtful. "We know one thing: We can't do magic when Mark is around but once the magic is done, he doesn't change it."

Harley made an impatient sound in his throat, loud enough to get everybody's attention. "Enough about coffee. Get back to telling us about Grayson."

Frank nodded. "We can still go out during daylight hours. The Guard rings the church bells to let us know when we can leave our homes. They ring them again to tell us when to return to our homes. If one of the Guard stops us we'd better have a good reason for being out and about. They prefer people to stay at home. The grocery stores still have staples and they bring in supplies but without trucks or trains running, it's a slow process.

"We receive allotments. Each family sends a representative to the store. This representative stands in line, receives the allotment, and that is all the family gets for that day. So far, the rationing has been equal and fair but as the supplies dwindle, there is lobbying for position. And there have been cases of attacks on individuals walking home, and their allotment stolen. Injuries are becoming common and seem to be getting increasingly more severe."

Frank took another sip of coffee, frowning into the tiny campfire before continuing. "Doctors, nurses, and anybody with any type of medical training are being pulled away from their jobs. Once they leave their jobs we don't see them again. In some cases entire families are gone. The lack of medical care is why we applied for, and received, permission to bring May and John to our house. We're planning on removing them from the nursing home tomorrow."

Harley nodded. "That's good. Once everybody is in one place we'll figure out a plan to get everybody out and back to the farm. So far we're enough off the beaten path that nobody has bothered us."

Frank eyed the horses. "I have to be back home by tomorrow morning. I don't want to risk the horses being seen. The military will confiscate them. You're lucky you didn't lose the horses when you approached the roadblock."

He handed his empty mug back to Shelly and stood up. "We'll go see if Mr. Higgins has a usable wagon. If he does we'll be one step closer to freedom."

Chapter 15

"I'm going home with you." Mark looked as stubborn as Bo had ever seen him. Uncle Frank looked uncertain.

"I don't know how we'd explain you," Frank said. "I'm not kidding, the soldiers are jumpy. Something is happening that I don't understand." Frank dropped to his heels by the little campfire. He reached for the ever-present pot of coffee. Flicker filled bowls with soup and handed them to Frank and Harley. "How did the meeting with Mr. Higgens go?"

Frank smiled his thanks for the soup, setting the bowl on the ground to cool while he drank his coffee. "Mr. Higgens has an old wagon. One of the wheels was cracked and the harness isn't in very good shape. Cosmos showed up." Frank smiled at Flicker. "I don't know how you contacted him, but thank you. He stayed behind to do the repairs." He set his coffee cup down and picked up the soup.

Harley took over updating Flicker and the children. "He agreed to give us the wagon and harness. Actually, his exact words were we could have the wagon if we'd trade a bred cow for it. He's more concerned about food for the winter than he is about an old horse-drawn wagon. He hasn't owned horses in twenty years so it's a useless item for him. He wants food. When Cosmos explained to him about the changes…" Harley grinned and Frank choked on the soup. "You had to be there." Harley shook his head. "Mr. Higgins's reaction to Cosmos, and magic, was a sight I won't soon forget.

"Anyway," Harley continued. "He asked for food. Fruits like apples, peaches, and pears. He wants flour, twenty-five or thirty pounds of it. And root vegetables, like carrots, potatoes, and squash. We give him food, we get the wagon."

He nodded toward a stack of baskets and containers. "If you kids could fill those, we'll get them back to Mr. Higgens.

Flicker nodded in understanding. "No problem. It's good practice for the girls." She motioned to Shelly and Eden. They pulled the containers across the clearing, away from Mark, and began gathering sticks, stones, and anything else that could be turned into food.

"Bo, Mark," she called out. "You can help by filling this big plastic container with dirt."

The boys nodded. Harley pulled a small garden trowel out of his bag, giving it to Mark to dig dirt with. He shrugged at their good-natured teasing. "Be glad I have it or you'd find yourself digging with rocks or sticks."

Frank listened to Harley and the boys but his attention was on the girls. Curiosity drove him to his feet. Coffee mug in hand, he walked over to watch. Flicker and Eden produced food with rapid ease. Shelly took a bit longer but her container held a respectable amount of potatoes, carrots, and apples.

Frank sank down on his heels again, apparently a favorite position, and reached for a round, rosy apple.

He took a cautious bite. His face lit up. "It looks like an apple, tastes like an apple, so it must be an apple. How do you do this again?"

Flicker explained. "It's mind over matter. The unstable magic that came through the rip in the sky contains atoms the mind can manipulate. If you believe strongly enough, the atoms will create what you will it to be."

Frank frowned and picked up a rock from the pile sitting in front of Shelly. He frowned in concentration. The rock remained a rock.

"Why can't I make something?" He glanced at Flicker. "I did exactly what you told me to do."

She smiled. "I'm sorry. We've found children still have the ability to believe with heart and soul. As they move toward adulthood, the mind begins to develop logic and no matter how much you want that rock to be an apple, you still believe it's a rock. You've gotten too old to make believe. I really am sorry. If adults could learn to focus, your world might not suffer such cataclysmic changes."

She leaned forward and plucked the rock from Frank's hand. Holding it at eye level she stared at it. A glistening, juicy something appeared in her hand. She handed it back to him. "This is a delicacy from my world. I give it to you. Let me know what you think of it."

Frank bit into the rich, purple flesh. His blue eyes sparkled and he smiled in delight. "It tastes like peaches and raspberries rolled into one. I like this a lot."

"I'm glad." Flicked nodded. The boys dragged the plastic container, now filled to the brim with dirt, over to the girls. Mark retreated to the other side of the clearing.

Flicked nodded her thanks to the boys before turning to Eden. "Change the container of dirt to the grain you use for bread."

Eden nodded. The five-gallon plastic container in front of her soon held flour. She put the lid on but couldn't seem to get it tight. Shelly leaned over and fixed it.

"There," Shelly said with a nod. "We've filled all the containers with every kind of food we can think of."

"Why no meat?" Frank asked. "Or eggs?"

Three frowning faces glowered at him. Eden responded, her voice stern. "Uncle Frank, the very first rule of magic is: What breathes, and bleeds, and procreates, magic must not duplicate."

Flicker smiled proudly at the little girl. She leaned toward Frank and spoke in a low voice. "Eden made a big mistake when magic first came to her. She's very careful not to break any magical laws."

Frank nodded. "I can see it will take time for me to catch up on the whole story. Right now, we need to figure out how to get this food to the Higgins farm. We'll take the horses with us, get the wagon hooked up, and bring it back here."

He stood up. "I'll help get the food where it needs to go and get the wagon hooked up and brought back here. Then I need to be home before daylight. I need to be standing in line at the grocery store by second bell or we won't get our allotment of food. And somebody would notice. We don't want anybody noticing us for any reason. By mid-morning I need to be at the nursing home to get May and John released to my custody."

Mark stood up, facing his father. "I'm going with you. I

don't care if I have to hide in the basement but I want to be home. You'll need help with Grandma and Grandpa." He glanced at the others, and a faint note of bitterness colored his voice. "It's obvious I'm not doing much good here."

Frank's face tightened, rejecting Mark's words, at the same time clearly wanting his son to be with him. Finally he sighed, ran his hand through his hair, and conceded. "Let's get things in order and then we'll discuss it., anyway, so we can have them pull the wagon back here."

Flicker stood up, "I'll call Cosmos in. He'll most likely have the repairs finished at the Higgins farm and you could use his help transporting this much food. Cos can use magic to levitate the containers and put protections on everything so nobody will see you."

"He can if I'm not with them." Mark's eyes darkened and his voice went mulish. "I'll stay here and help protect Edie. But I am going home with you." He glared at his father before turning away to help saddle the horses.

Chapter 16

"Wait up, boy. I need to rest." Hemlock stumbled and cursed. Powerful in magic, she wished she dared use magic to give her back a youthful, strong body. But using forbidden magic would bring the Executioner down on her faster than breathing. Someday, though. She gazed unseeingly into space, projecting herself into a future where she'd be young, and beautiful, and even more powerful than she was now. She would no longer have to be dependent only on magic. She squashed down the anger she felt thinking about Dalt. Someday she wouldn't need his help. She'd cast off the weakness age had brought to her.

Dalt moved into her line of sight. Her beautiful vision of youth and energy crumpled.

Unfailingly kind and gentle, Dalt patted her shoulder. "Do you want me to carry you?"

"No." Her words came out angry and rude. "I don't want you to carry me. I want you to find me a soft place to sit and fix me something to eat."

Dalt nodded. He found a small hillock perfect for sitting on. He carefully hollowed the top and lined it with fresh grasses. Hemlock had warned him against using even the simplest of magic. Truth be told, simple magic was all he was capable of.

He returned to Hemlock and, despite her words, scooped her into his arms. He cradled her, walking with soft, easy steps to the seat he had prepared for her. In his arms, he treated her like a delicate china cup he'd held as a boy, one that had shattered in his hands and earned him a harsh blow across his face. Dalt remembered the lessons he'd learned at the price of pain.

"I'm hungry, Dalt." Only in front of Dalt would Hemlock show weakness. His devotion to her never wavered. She knew it would never occur to the man to betray her.

He busied himself making sure of her comfort, then rocked back on his heels. "What do you want me to hunt for?"

She knew from experience that Dalt needed explicit instructions. "Do you remember the berries Ian picked? See if you can find some of those. If not, those red fruits we saw yesterday were very good."

Dalt smiled, reached inside his shirt, and pulled out three red apples. "Are these the ones?"

Hemlock's lips turned upward. Her green eyes remained hard. "Yes, boy. Those are the ones." She reached out and took all three.

Dalt rose to his feet with an ease she envied. When she moved, every bone she owned creaked and popped. "You go find more food, boy. I'll sit here and rest."

He nodded and turned to follow their path back to the fruit trees. He might not be bright, but he was observant. She knew he would find and gather food. He might not talk much but he took excellent care of her. She'd keep him around as long as he proved useful.

Her teeth were no longer strong enough to bite into the crisp flesh of the red fruit, so she pulled out her small eating knife and sliced thin pieces off. It made eating slower, but she enjoyed the white flesh. The juice felt good on her parched tongue. If only they weren't being hunted by the Executioner, she could grow to like this world they'd been thrown into.

She heard the snapping of twigs and a rustling of bushes. Hemlock placed the last sliver of fruit into her mouth, brushing the seeds and scraps from her as she slowly stood up. Dalt had never been this noisy, not even at his clumsiest. A stranger crashed into the clearing. Wild-eyed panic poured from him. Hemlock, eyes cold and unblinking, watched him.

She recognized the moment he realized her presence. At first, she thought he'd bolt from the clearing. He stopped, looking her over from head to toe. She saw him glance at the little eating knife she still held and knew the moment he dismissed it, and her, as non-threatening. She did her best to look helpless.

He jabbered at her in the language the children used. She hadn't understood it then. She made no effort to comprehend it now. She didn't care what the man wanted. She only cared about her needs. And right now she needed knowledge of this world.

Hemlock weighed her needs against the risk. She'd be long gone from this area before Cosmos could locate her position. She raised her hands and used forbidden magic.

Chapter 17

"Tell me again why we're sitting in a tree." Bo leaned forward so he could peer through the leaves at Mark. Both boys sat in an old oak tree growing behind Mr. Petersen's backyard fence. Mark sat on a limb that gave him a view of Petersen's yard.

Bo heard Mark sigh, but in the deepening darkness before nightfall, Mark's face blurred against the leafy branches.

"Because I know my father. I'm betting he left the group before they got all the way back to the clearing so he wouldn't have to tell me I couldn't go home with him. He would have never given me the opportunity to ask again."

Bo didn't speak. He didn't know what to say to Mark's words. Would his dad have done the same thing? Considering the fact both boys now sat in a tree this close to the Grayson epicenter, he suspected not, but how could he say for certain? A father worried about his children and Uncle Frank hadn't witnessed the children in action against a very scary renegade named Dragen.

"What if you're wrong? Won't your dad be mad when he gets to the clearing and finds you gone?"

"Don't worry about it," Mark muttered. "I know what I'm doing, Bo. You can go back to the clearing if you want. I'm going home tonight but you don't have to come. You probably shouldn't anyway. Dad's argument is they can't explain me being there so how in the world would they explain you?"

Bo shrugged. "You heard Flicker. She said nobody goes anywhere alone. She's been working with both of us on self-defense. We're no match physically for Dalt but we could take out the old woman."

"Unless she turned us into toads," Mark murmured. "She's not too worried about breaking the laws of magic."

Bo laughed. "Won't she be surprised if she tries to use magic on you?"

"I never thought of that." Mark sounded thoughtful. In the dim light Bo couldn't see his face clearly enough to tell. "I hear Dad coming," Mark whispered.

"I hope its Uncle Frank." Bo hunched himself into as small a figure as he could manage perched on a tree branch. Mark followed suit, almost disappearing from sight among the thick leaves on the tree.

The tall man was a blur as he moved through the deep dusk. Before he could vault over the fence Mark spoke. "Hold up, Dad. I'm going with you." Without further words, Mark hung from the branch and dropped lightly to the ground.

Bo followed, hitting the ground with a hard thud that rattled his teeth. He stood up and positioned himself slightly behind Mark.

"Mark." A few half-swallowed swear words followed. Bo slid a few steps to the side and watched his cousin face down his uncle. The sight of the tall man and the half-grown youth facing off against each other gave Bo a distinctly unsettled feeling.

He remembered Silas's and Flicker's warning that he and Mark, still considered children in their culture, would become Hunters in this new world that would rapidly evolve. He could envision the change happening as he watched Mark go toe to toe with Frank.

Frank looked grim and his voice raised the hair on Bo's arms. "You and Bo need to return to the clearing. I'm not exposing you to the chaos in Grayson right now."

"Dad, Bo and I know what's happening. We know why it's happening. We can recognize both Dalt and Hemlock. You and mom need help to get Grandma and Grandpa out of town."

Bo spoke before he thought, adding strength to Mark's argument. "We're strong, Uncle Frank. And we're not afraid to work. You think of us as boys but we've had to grow up fast."

Mark and his father swiveled their heads to stare at him and Bo wished he'd kept his mouth shut. Mark looked hopeful. Uncle Frank scowled. "Explain what you mean."

Mark sounded stubborn. "You weren't there when Dragen took Eden. We had to rescue her. All of us, working together with the Hunters. You saw Cosmos. You know changes are coming. Mark and I are being trained to be Hunters in our own world."

"Don't be silly," Frank protested. "Bo just turned fourteen. Your birthday isn't until October. You need to finish high school, go to college. Train for a real job you can earn a living at."

Sadness deepened Mark's voice. "Dad, you've seen Grayson. Is anybody working, or living, in a normal manner right now?"

Bo could tell his uncle didn't like the reality of Mark's words. Frank's head shake was so infinitesimal Bo almost missed it.

Mark spoke again. "Grayson is the beginning. We're lucky, because we met with Cosmos, Flicker, and Silas. We saw first-hand what the change does. We can learn, and adjust, fast enough to help others."

Bo broke in. "Please, Uncle Frank. Can't we just go to your house and talk about this inside? I'm getting really nervous about military patrols."

"Or worse," Mark added. "Mr. Petersen might let his dog out." The words no more than left his mouth when they heard the sound of a door opening followed by the high-pitched bark of a little dog.

Without a word, Bo dug in his pocket and pulled out the small bag holding the happy powder they had used earlier.

A short time later, with a minimum of giggling, swearing, and running, they fell through the back door into the kitchen and faced a far bigger wrath than Mr. Petersen's little dog: Aunt Claire. Bo wished he dared use the happy powder on her.

"Where have you been?" Claire locked the back door. Then scurried around the room making sure the curtains were pulled shut. The lone candle sitting in the center of the kitchen table didn't give off much light.

Bo watched his aunt give Frank a hard kiss. Then she grabbed Mark and pulled him into a tight embrace. He was startled when she did the same to him. Who would guess Aunt Claire had a grip that could choke a horse?

She let him loose, talking all the while. "How could you make me wait so long? I was terrified a soldier would come to the door asking for you. Or worse, tell me you'd been found dead. I've been going out of my mind with worry. Wondering how I'd get Mom and Dad out of the nursing home and back here all by myself."

Frank wrapped his arm around her shoulder, putting a gentle hand over her mouth. "Hush, Claire. Shh. We're here. We'll all go to sleep and get up early. Right now we're tired. And it's late. Let's bed the boys down. Tomorrow we'll talk."

Aunt Claire gave a shaky head nod and managed a watery smile at the boys. Bo gave her credit for not crying in front of them.

***

"Stay away from the breaker box," Bo warned Mark.

"Why is that?" Frank snapped the legs of the cot into place. He moved aside while Claire put blankets and pillow in place.

"We told you how magic works," Mark replied. "But we found out that I nullify magic. Where I am, magic isn't. Cosmos took me to a deserted house and when I stood next to the breaker box the electricity worked normally."

His father frowned as he thought about Mark's words. "Son, don't you go telling anybody about that. There are a lot of frightened people out there who want their lives to go back to normal. If they find out you can keep the magic away, you're in danger."

Mark said, "That's sort of what Cosmos told me. I'm hoping there will be others like me."

Frank nodded in agreement. The cots were ready and the boys were tired. Claire and Frank hugged them both and told them to go to sleep. Frank stood a moment, looking hard at each boy. "Whatever you do, don't go upstairs for any reason."

The boys nodded. He would get no argument from them. The cots were hard, the pillows soft, and the day had been brutally long. They fell asleep as soon as they stretched out.

Chapter 18

"You can't go with me." Frank glared over the rim of his coffee cup at Mark. "The soldiers are nervous. I don't want them grabbing you, or worse, shooting at you."

Claire handed granola bars and fruit to the boys, stopping briefly behind Mark to stroke his hair. "Please, Mark. You don't understand how life has been here. The strangest things are happening. Creatures that should never exist roam the streets. Strange objects fly through the air. The townspeople are afraid the soldiers will start shooting at anything that moves."

Frank set his cup of coffee on the table. "Just last week, one of the soldiers shot a basketball out of the air. Granted it was hanging in the air above a telephone pole but still, they shouldn't have shot at all."

Mark frowned, thinking hard. "I think I know what's happening. Adults don't seem to be able to access the magic that came through the rip in the sky but children, young enough to not completely understand the difference between real and make-believe, are able to create whatever they think of."

Claire sat down at the table. "That would explain a lot. There have been rumors of…" She searched for the right words. "…strange creatures being found under beds, and in closets. Creatures that can't possibly be real except they move, and apparently die. Anything strange that is found, captured, or destroyed is taken to the gymnasium at the school. Nobody is allowed near the school except for a handful of scientists who have been brought in to examine everything."

Frank interrupted his wife. "The creatures don't seem to move in a normal manner. They only make certain movements, or sounds, as if by rote. I'm assuming, from what you kids just told us, the creatures are made up in the children's own minds. They only do what the child perceives they should do?"

Mark and Bo nodded.

Claire added, "Some families are eating better than others. The children must have learned how to create food to eat. And nobody really talks about it because how can any of this be possible? It's crazy. The whole world has gone mad."

"Not the whole world." Bo swallowed. "Just Grayson."

Mark added, "You'll have to give it time before it's the whole world. The magic will spread as the wind blows."

Frank's face turned grim. He turned a reproving look on the boys. "It sounds crazy but we know it's real. Claire…" He turned to look at his wife. "You and I need to get your parents. I'm not sure how we'll get your father home. A wheelchair will probably be our best bet. Your mom gets around fairly well except she tends to wander off. You stay with her. I'll push your dad and we'll get back here as soon as we can."

He stood up. "You boys stay in the house. Don't open the doors. Don't look out the windows. I can't stress hard enough how jumpy the soldiers are. If they see movement where there isn't supposed to be any they will shoot first and ask questions later. We're living under martial law right now and the soldiers make the rules.

Mark nodded and locked the door behind his parents. He stood at the door with his head bowed, forehead touching the cool wood. Then he straightened and looked at Bo. "No sense worrying. What we can do is get ready. Let's tidy the house up for Mom. We'll look around and see if there is anything here that needs to be taken to the farm. To be honest, Bo, I'm more afraid of escaped convicts than I am trigger-happy soldiers."

Bo nodded. "I agree. Life is going to get really crazy before it gets better. I hope Silas gets back soon with the hunters and teachers so we can get some order back. At least get some of us trained so we can spread out and help as the change spirals outward."

The boys busied themselves cleaning. There wasn't a lot to do. Claire was a meticulous housekeeper.

***

"Stop complaining." Hemlock glared at the man. "If you continue to cluck and annoy me, I'll give you a reason to cluck."

The man, Spider, choked mid-sentence. He'd seen the old woman in action. With one wave of her hand she'd changed him. He didn't feel any different but the words coming out of his mouth were no longer in English. "I should have killed you the minute I laid eyes on you." Rage fueled him, and he balled his fists.

Hemlock laughed. "As if you could. You don't understand what's happened, do you? Your world is changing. The

very air you breathe is different. I hold power in my hands."
She held her hands up and fire leaped from her fingers.

Her hands, yes, but the focus, the ring she had taken
such care in creating, held nothing. The extra power she'd
always counted on was now gone. Dalt must never realize
her focus was useless. She wouldn't risk diminishing his
respect and fear of her.

The magic was altering this world, but this world was
also changing the magic. The old ways she had counted
on weren't working. It was imperative she figure out the
new rules as rapidly as she could.

Spider tried, once again, to reason with her. "I don't
want to go back to Grayson. You don't understand. I
escaped from there. If I go back they'll lock me up again.
Or worse, shoot me on sight."

Rage shook the old woman. She wanted nothing more
than to shrink the man to bug size and then stomp on him
and grind him into the ground. It had been years since
anyone had questioned her actions.

She stood up, ignoring the pain in her joints, and
walked toward the man. He had sense enough to cower.
"You will do what I say…" Closer she stepped. He shrank
away from her, his feet pinned to the ground.

"…when I say." Close enough now, she jabbed a finger
into the man's chest.

"You will take us to this town you call Grayson. I
control magic. I will be in charge and nobody will stand
against me."

She ignored the image of Cosmos in his full power.
She'd deal with him later. She had plenty of time to think
on her way to Grayson.

The wild magic swirling around Grayson would fuel her power. When she regained control of the girl, she could carry that power wherever she went.

She glared into Spider's brown, angry eyes. "Get me to Grayson and I'll set you free."

Chapter 19

"Get away from the window," Bo warned his cousin. "Uncle Frank specifically told us to stay hidden."

Mark pulled back from the one-inch slit of curtain. "They're late. If they don't get here in the next few minutes, I'm going after them."

"No, you won't." Bo moved into the stance Uncle Harley had taught him was best for self-defense. "I won't let you near the door."

Before the last word left his mouth the front door banged open. Frank and Claire spilled into the living room. Frank, looking wild-eyed, his hair standing on end, slammed the door shut and slid the deadbolt into place.

Mark deserted his post at the window and ran to his mother's side. Her wind-blown hair swirled wildly around her face. Exertion had turned her face beet red.

Frank pushed his glasses back into place. He ran a hand over his hair, smoothing it back into place. "Boys?" He straightened up. "We need a Plan B." With that he strode past them heading for the kitchen.

Claire followed him.

Bo grabbed Mark's arm. "Plan B? What happened to Plan A?"

Mark shook him off, and loped toward the kitchen. He skidded to a stop to avoid being run over by his father's pacing.

"What happened?" He sidled toward his mother sitting at the kitchen table. Silent tears slid down her face, adding to Mark's worry.

"Somebody tell us something." Bo darted behind Frank as he turned to pace the other direction. He sat down opposite Claire and Mark.

"Oh, Frank!" Claire wailed. Mark leaned over and pulled the last sheet off the paper towel dispenser. He handed the towel to his mother. She gave him a teary smile. He awkwardly patted her shoulder.

"Dad. Sit." Mark used his foot to slide a chair out, effectively blocking his father's movement. "We need to know what happened."

A timid knock on the back door sent a look of horror over Frank's face. Without a word, Bo and Mark, taking time to push their chairs under the table, bolted for the living room.

They didn't get far. The sound of Frank cussing and Shelly's voice brought them back to the kitchen as fast as they'd left it.

"What are you doing here?" Bo frowned at his younger sister. "Where is Eden? You didn't lose her, did you?"

Shelly glared at him. "Of course we didn't lose Edie." A smile of pure delight lit her face. "Cosmos flew me here. He used some sort of cloaking device so we wouldn't be seen. He dropped me in the yard, then went back to help Harley get the horses moved. Flicker is bringing Edie. It took them longer because they had to come by foot." She wiggled in excitement. "Cosmos can fly, Bo. In the air."

"Why wouldn't he?" Mark glowered at her. "He's light. Light can go anywhere."

Bo shoved his cousin lightly, almost politely, because Frank and Claire were in the room and he didn't want to get scolded. "Quit asking her stupid questions. I want to know what happened. Why are you all coming here? Uncle Frank told us not to be here and now everybody is coming?"

"That's what I want to know." Frank waved at the girl. "Sit. Talk."

Shelly gulped so hard Bo could see it. She sank onto the chair Frank pulled out for her. Claire jumped to her feet. "I don't have much to offer. I do have some hot chocolate mix that can be made with water. You talk while I get the chocolate ready." She hurried to the stove to reheat the water from the morning's breakfast.

Shelly opened her mouth to speak when another soft tap sounded at the back door. Frank sighed; Bo and Mark stayed in their chairs, waiting for Frank to answer the door.

He peeked through the crack before swinging the door wide. "Is anybody else showing up?"

Flicker smiled, shy as a bird. "Cosmos will be here soon. He went back to the clearing to do a final check on the wagon and harness. When he's sure everything is in order, he'll leave Harley to keep watch while he comes back here to help us relocate you and your parents."

Frank glowered. Mark spoke. "You said we needed a Plan B. Looks like Plan B has arrived."

Bo leaned back as Claire placed a cup of steaming hot chocolatein front of him. He smiled his thanks. "I bet you're glad Uncle Frank won the generator argument."

His aunt smiled and ruffled his hair, just as he'd seen her do so often to Mark. "The hard part was getting propane. We were on city gas but Frank managed to get us set up with some fuel. We're careful how often we use it but we figured we'd be relocated to the farm before we ran out. It's getting low. There's not much left and no way to get more."

Bo smiled at her again before turning back to Flicker and Eden. He had questions but before he could ask them, Eden launched herself at him.

She climbed into his lap and hugged him tight. "I missed you, Bo."

He hugged her back. "I missed you, too, squirt. Now go sit on your own chair."

She pulled back, her blue eyes sparkling, her fine-textured blond hair curling and flying wildly from static electricity. Before he could protest, she kissed his cheek and wiggled back to the floor.

She headed for Mark. Bo's heart ached to see the struggle it took for her to move through the barrier of Mark's anti-magic shield that surrounded him. Eden stopped, and a look of grim determination that usually struck a chord of terror in him crossed her face.

"Markie, pull it in. I'll do the same."

"Pull what in?" Mark looked confused.

Bo could see the little girl concentrating. He said, "I think she's trying to pull into herself whatever attracts the magic. She wants you to try to pull into yourself whatever it is that repels the magic."

Understanding lit Mark's eyes. "Okay, I'll give it a try."

The others watched. Flicker's eyes betrayed her intense interest in the process. With an almost audible 'pop' the little girl fell forward into Mark's arms. She immediately crawled onto his lap and hugged him tight.

"We did it, Markie. We'll remember how we did it so I can give you hugs."

He smiled down at his young cousin and ruffled her already wild hair, sending it to even greater heights. "We did it, munchkin. I wouldn't have thought about pulling it in. But I think it might be a good idea for you to move because I don't think I'm going to be able to hold it in much longer."

She nodded. "I know." She kissed his cheek and hopped down. "But we'll get better at it."

Mark exhaled, and the little girl moved away from him faster than she'd intended as Mark's repel sent her skidding toward Flicker.

"Whoa, Eden." Flicker lifted the little girl up onto the bar stool. Claire set a cup of hot chocolate in front of Eden. The little girl smiled at her aunt.

"That was interesting." Flicker smoothed Eden's hair, calming the electricity. "The magic is mutating in your world. In ways we've never seen before. This is going to create a multitude of problems for our hunters and teachers."

Bo agreed. And it was still summer. What would happen when winter came and the furnaces wouldn't work? How could people survive the harsh temperatures without electricity? How fast would the magic spread? "I want to know what happened at the nursing home, Uncle Frank. Where are Grandma and Grandpa?"

Claire started to cry again. Frank sighed and sat down on the second bar stool next to Eden. "Your grandfather is bedridden. I thought we could put him in a wheelchair to transport him home. The nursing home is chaos. Pure and simple. There are… things… roaming the halls."

"Things that should never exist," Claire burst out. "I ran past something that looked like a teddy bear, only it moved and spoke to me." She sounded horrified and Bo had to agree that a talking teddy bear would be strange.

"Some sort of…" Claire struggled for words. "…monster is the only way I can describe it, sort of Frankenstein's monster and Dracula mixed into one being… It pinned your father to the wall. He had to fight it but when he punched it, whatever it was, vanished as if it had never been there. Bugs were crawling on the walls, and nightmarish things I could only see out of the corner of my eyes. When I looked directly at them, nothing was there." She cried harder and Mark pushed the paper towel lying on the table toward her.

"I ran to your grandfather's room and there he was, sleeping. Oblivious to everything. I couldn't lift him up. Mother wasn't in the room so I sent Frank looking for her. He found her and brought her back. She was holding a bouquet of beautiful flowers and didn't seem to be aware of the horrible things going on."

Bo leaned toward Mark and spoke under his breath. "Knowing the state of Grandma's brain, she was probably responsible for half of them."

Mark didn't look at him but managed to give Bo a painful toe stomp. That's all he could manage without risking his Dad's disapproval.

Claire cried harder. Frank took over the story. "Nobody seemed to be in charge. The residents who could still get around were getting into everything. Even rooms I know should have been off-limits didn't stop them. Doors that I know are kept locked, were standing open. I saw one door open for someone without anybody touching it. The whole place was pure chaos."

Frank's voice went grim. "I was looking for a wheel-chair so we could move Dad when soldiers entered the building. They carried weapons and ordered us to leave. I showed them the discharge papers and they told us we'd have to come back later. They weren't going to let us take John and May with us, so we had to leave without them."

Claire burst out, "I'm not going to the farm without them. I want them out of that chaos. It's horrible. I want to take them home."

Flicker started to speak. A sharp knock, followed by the kitchen door opening, halted her. Cosmos stepped into the room. He held his fingers to his lips, a seemingly universal sign for quiet. He held a box up and fiddled with the dials. Finally, he nodded. "Okay. I can talk now."

Bo had seen Cosmos's eyes show many different things but this time all he saw was black. No stars, no moons, no comets. He swallowed a giggle and whispered to Mark, "He must be in stealth mode."

Mark choked. He reached for his hot chocolate and gulped, trying to swallow the wild laughter threatening to erupt.

When Cosmos spoke, Bo reached for his own mug. It was impossible to tell whether Cosmos looked at them or even guessed at the boys' struggle to contain themselves. "I've put your house under a cloak of invisibility. Anybody seeking you will not see the house. They will be compelled to look away from it. This is technology and not affected by Mark's ability to nullify magic."

Flicker frowned at Cosmos. "Why didn't we do this in the clearing? Maybe we wouldn't have had to abandon the campsite."

Cosmos's eyes lightened. Still gray, a hint of sunshine threatened to peek through. "I did say alien technology, didn't I?"

Mark blurted out, "You didn't break a rule, did you, Cos?"

The gray parted and sunlight peeked through in Cosmos's eyes. "I bent the rules, just a little bit, young Mark. Sometimes necessity results in actions one might otherwise not do."

"I'll remember that," Mark warned.

"You do that, Mark."

Sunlight burst through the gray in Cosmos eyes and for a little while Earth seemed safe and normal.

Chapter 20

"Why do you want to go to Grayson anyway?" Spider scowled at the old woman.

She scowled back. Her eyes glittered with anger and malice. "Magic. We fell into your world right above this town you call Grayson. In time, the magic will spread across your world but right now, the largest amount of magic is strongest in Grayson. If I can get closer I can access and control it."

Spider rocked back on his heels, eying the old woman with curiosity. "You can keep me from being arrested? Keep me from being locked up?" His eyes slid to Dalt, taking in the size and strength of the big man. He recognized the calm obedience in Dalt. The man wouldn't do anything unless the old woman told him to. He presented no immediate threat.

"I don't know what this word, arrest, means. If you explain it to me, I'm sure I can prevent it happening to you." Hemlock waved her hand, dismissing the subject.

He tried to explain. "My world has cages. When we do something that others don't like, we are arrested and put into the cages."

Hemlock frowned, remembering her own incarceration inside the nullifier. Being locked up was the reason Dragen had led them to exile into a world without magic. For a few moments she thought about the punishment she would do to Dragen if he was here. Then she let the image go. Dragen was being punished far more severely than anything she could devise. "Your world is strange to me. I could use guidance while I take control of your town."

Spider cocked his head, weighing Hemlock's words. She was so frail, he could snap her like a twig. His mouth tightened. She could also turn him *into* a twig. He'd seen the magic she wielded. "All right. I believe you can do what you say you can do. I'll guide you into town and help you understand our way of life. In return, you will ensure I stay free?"

She nodded. "Not only free, but I'll reward you. Whatever you ask for, I'll make sure you get."

Dalt glanced down at Hemlock. A strange look flicked through his eyes, gone in a flash. He went back to watching Spider with stolid indifference.

"What do we do first?" Spider asked.

Hemlock gazed into the distance, deep in thought. "First, I need you to sleep." She waved a hand at him. Spider crumpled to the ground.

She turned her head and looked at Dalt, a long measuring survey. "I need you to go into the woods and hunt for food."

He nodded in calm acceptance of her words. Without a sound or a word, he left the clearing.

Hemlock rose and started to hunt through the grass and leaves. "One rock," she muttered. "One small stone. Something from this world. My focus is useless here but maybe that's because it's alien to this world. The magic is mutating. Maybe if I use a stone that belongs on this world. Maybe then I can hold power in my hands again. I need more than the wild magic. I need it all."

Madness glittered in her faded eyes. She muttered and cursed. Finally, on her hands and knees, she found the perfect stone. With Spider sleeping and Dalt away, she created a receptacle for magic. All the magic required was an object from its own world. *Made sense, really,* she thought. *Earth is imposing its own rules on magic. The magic in this place requires elements that belong to Earth. I should have thought of this sooner.*

Long before Dalt returned and Spider woke up, Hemlock wore a new focus, safe in an amulet bag on a ribbon around her neck.

Chapter 21

"You're sure the soldiers will stay away from the house?" Frank frowned at the kitchen full of people.

"I'm sure." Cosmos nodded. "This is technology used on my worlds. Terra will be no different."

"Earth," Eden corrected.

A warm sun rose in Cosmos's left eye. Soft fluffy clouds floated in his right. His eyes always looked warm and gentle when he looked at Eden.

"Earth," he repeated. "It would be best if we get you out of Grayson before the day is over."

Bo slouched on his chair and watched Aunt Claire start shaking her head before Cosmos finished his sentence.

"No." She turned to Frank. "I won't leave without my parents. I won't."

Uncle Frank ran his hands through his hair, then readjusted his glasses. "Take the children back to the farm. Claire and I will work to get her parents out of the nursing home. We'll follow when able."

Mark protested. "I'm not leaving you here. I won't go." Bo could tell from Mark's stubborn jaw clench he wasn't going to budge. If Cosmos expected them to get Mark back to the farm, they'd have to physically carry him. Preferably bound and gagged.

"What is the problem getting your parents released?" Cosmos sounded curious. Dark gray fog swirled in his eyes.

"We tried." Tears welled up in Claire's face. Shelly pulled a dry, clean hanky out of her pocket and handed it to her aunt.

Eden slid off her chair and went to lean against Claire's side. She patted her aunt's arm. "There, there, Auntie Claire. Everything will be all right."

Flicker, leaning against the kitchen counter, eyed the woman. Bo could tell, from the short time he'd known the girl that she was deep in thought and running scenarios through her head.

Claire waved a hand at her husband before pressing the hanky to her eyes.

Frank nodded at his wife and explained. "We went to get John and May this morning. John is bedridden from a stroke. I thought we could put him in a wheelchair to bring him home. May is suffering from dementia. She's physically functional but it's hard to keep track of her. Her mind wanders and she's easily distracted. She still knows her husband. I thought she would go where he went."

Frank sighed. Bo could tell from the look on his face what he said next would be grim. "Claire and I weren't able to lift her father into the wheelchair. He's dead weight and we just couldn't get him up and positioned. Then the disturbances began."

"They were horrible." Claire lowered the cloth to look at Flicker and Cosmos. "Creatures that should never exist. Scary, horrible, frightening beings. Swooping at us. Clawing at us. They didn't bother my parents. It seemed like the old folks didn't even see them. And the creatures ignored them right back."

Claire's voice sank to a rasping whisper. "I saw something crawl past the door of the room. Dark, ugly, slithering on its belly. It stopped and peered in at us. I could see it looking at us before it went on to the next room. A few minutes later I heard an agonizing scream come from a few doors down. I know it went in there. I just know it."

Bo noticed everyone in the room leaning forward, hanging onto Claire's words. He rotated his shoulder and forced himself to sit back in his chair.

Flicker nodded, her face resolute. "It's not uncommon for those afflicted to have waking nightmares. I didn't expect it to be this way on your Earth. I thought only young children would be affected by the change, and your world would adapt as the children grew up. I was wrong."

Cosmos nodded. "It's obvious that this place where your parents are is experiencing the results of the contamination. We will spend the rest of today preparing. Gather the things you wish to take to the farm. I'll move everything to the wagon so Harley can load up and be ready to travel tomorrow."

Cosmos moved toward the kitchen door leading outdoors. He stood, one hand on the knob. "We'll all go together to get your parents. We won't be coming back here. Once we get past the roadblock, we'll meet up with Harley. He'll have the wagon and horses ready for travel. We'll be back at the farm before the week is over."

At his words, Claire began crying in earnest. Frank pulled her to his feet and wrapped her in a big hug. Mark went to them and his father pulled him in.

Bo rocked back on his chair, confident Aunt Claire wouldn't notice and scold him. Operation Rescue Grandparents, under the command of Cosmos, surely wouldn't fail.

Chapter 22

"How are we going to get past the soldiers?" Spider leaned over and spoke in Hemlock's ear. "When we broke out of jail we left a few bodies on the ground. They might shoot me on sight."

Hemlock stroked her new amulet bag. Power was hers again. Her success in creating a new focus using a stone from Earth gave her confidence.

"We'll have to make sure they don't see us." She held her hands up, forming an 'O' and into the circle she sent a 'see clearly' thought. Objects and people came sharply into focus. She took care to examine the weapons carried by the sentries.

"We'll enter tonight, after it's fully dark. Right now, we'll stay in the woods. Eat, rest, and prepare."

She turned and hobbled toward the tree line. Dalt hurried to her side and slipped a gentle hand under her elbow. Hemlock didn't thank him but she accepted his aid and wished she dared use her newly gathered magic to change her old and creaking body into a younger version.

Not yet, she thought. The Executioner is too close. Soon I'll do whatever I want without fear of retribution.

Chapter 23

The kitchen door opened and closed one last time. Cosmos had spent the night transporting the items Claire couldn't bear to leave behind: photos, keepsakes, a box of quilts and needlework. Frank's choices had been more practical: tools and a few books.

"We'll lock the house up tight." Flicker patted Claire's shoulder. "We'll put a Keep Away spell on the house and the yard. It should keep anybody from bothering your things until we can return."

Claire looked around the kitchen. The room felt warm and welcoming filled with people. Eden looked up from her breakfast, a bowl of fruit salad, and gave a heartbreakingly sweet smile at her aunt. "Don't worry. We'll make sure everything is safe before we leave."

"Thank you, Edie." Claire smiled back at the little girl. "That makes me feel better."

Eden scooped the last spoonful of fruit out of her bowl. Shelly snatched the bowl and put it in the soapy dishwater. Bo was on washing duty. Mark dried the dishes and put them away.

"What's the plan?" Frank held his cup of water out to Shelly. She smiled at him and left the room to return a few minutes later with a steaming cup of coffee. Mark's circle of un-magic now encompassed whatever room he stood in.

Frank smiled his thanks at her. "Of all the coffee I've drunk, I prefer yours. You put a special something into the flavor. I don't know what it is but it hits the spot."

She smiled back at him, a dimple flashing in one cheek. "I told you before. It's because the only coffee I've ever tasted was from Starbucks. It might not even exist except in my imagination."

"Well, be careful who you serve it to. You might find yourself being on coffee duty for the rest of your life."

His words wiped the smile off Shelly's face. What would she do with her life? According to Flicker children became hunters, or teachers. There were other duties, of course, but she hadn't been introduced to them. What kinds of jobs would be left on Earth once the change was complete?

"What's the plan?" Bo pulled the plug and the water drained out of the sink. Mark hung the damp dishtowel on the handle of the oven. Both boys turned toward Cosmos.

His gaze seemed bright, even for his strange eyes. Bo realized there was an actual light shining from them. Before he could say anything, Cosmos seemed to remember he was indoors and the light dimmed, replaced by something intense resembling the eyes of the far-seeing hawk.

"It was dark outside and I borrowed light to see by." He turned his attention to Frank and Claire. "The sun is up now so we should go where your parents are being held. You will present your papers and we'll bring them out with us."

"We tried that yesterday," Frank protested. "Why do you think that plan will work any better today?"

"Yesterday you didn't have Flicker and me. Today, you do." Cosmos shrugged one shoulder, his supreme confidence causing Bo to duck his head to hide the grin spreading over face. Mark punched Bo and managed to keep his own face expressionless.

Cosmos ignored the boys. "We will ensure the release of your parents. Nobody on your world understands how magic works. It would be better if we had a teacher with us. They are trained to help new magic wielders whereas Hunters are trained to capture and subdue the ones who willfully misuse magic. But I'm sure we can manage."

Frank cocked an eyebrow but didn't respond. Bo knew his uncle was withholding judgment until he saw Cosmos and Flicker in action. A warm feeling spread in his stomach. His uncle had never seen Shelly, Eden, and himself in action either. In a world rapidly changing, they were changing too.

***

"I don't think it's a good idea for all of us to go," Frank protested.

Bo had never seen his uncle look so determined.

Frank added, "The soldiers are jumpy. I don't trust them to hold their fire if the strange things we saw yesterday appear. Heck." His expression darkened. "If I'd been carrying a pistol there were a few apparitions I would have shot at."

Cosmos's eyes went stormy. "I understand your fears but we won't be coming back here. As soon as we get your parents out of this building they are being held in,

Flicker and I will get you out of the town. All of this will happen very quickly."

Claire slung one of Mark's old backpacks, containing the items she didn't want out of her possession, over her shoulder, muttering grimly, "There is no quick where Mother is concerned."

Flicker smiled and reached out to help Claire adjust the pack to a more comfortable position. "Please don't worry. I promise you we will handle things. Your parents won't be frightened or hurt."

They closed the front door. Frank tried the handle to make sure it was securely locked.

Mark edged closer to Bo. "Cosmos and Flicker do know what they're doing, right?"

Bo shrugged. "Have they steered us wrong yet?"

"No," Mark sighed. "But I've noticed that Earth isn't cooperating in ways they are familiar with. I have a feeling we're in for a few surprises along the way. And so are they."

Bo shrugged. "Then we'll deal with them. That's all we can…" He slid to a stop. "What the heck is that?"

The children pulled together into a huddle. Frank and Claire looked grim. Flicker looked puzzled. It was hard to read any expression on Cosmos's face, covered as it was by the black cloth. His eyes went completely black, then sharpened into the golden eagle's eyes that he seemed to be using more the longer he was on Earth.

They stood on the edge of Main Street. As far as the eye could see, strange animals walked and flew. Bright colored balloons in odd sizes and shapes floated in the air, sometimes moving and changing but never floating upward the way a normal, helium-filled balloon would.

"It looks like a parade dreamed up by a crazy person," Shelly whispered. She stepped closer to her aunt, seeking comfort.

"How do we get through that?" Mark asked. "Will the animals hurt us?"

Bo added, "Will we have to fight?"

Flicker looked uncertain. "Your world does not understand any of the rules of magic. These things are created by the imaginations of children too young to reason. There is no rhyme or reason to these creations."

An ice storm blew through Cosmos's eyes. "And most of them are highly illegal. I can't put judgment on children too young to reason. They have no concept of right and wrong yet. The teachers must come. The job ahead is daunting." He fell silent. His eyes remained icy and cold.

A bubble of laughter burst from Bo. He shoved Mark hard between the shoulder blades. "You take point. Walk about ten feet in front of us."

Mark spun around, horror on his face and in his voice. "Are you crazy?"

"No." Bo laughed harder. "Just do it. Cosmos will rescue you if one of the big, bad creatures tries to step on you."

Mark turned around, eyeing Main Street where a two-headed giraffe-elephant walked, and dog-cats yipped and hissed. Impossible animals that nature never intended capered and played in the street. None of them tried to leave, but milled and lumbered from curb to curb the length of Main Street.

Blocking both lanes, cars and trucks dotted the street like a crazy obstacle course.

Frank's voice sounded loud. Even with the noise made by the impossible animals, the lack of anything motorized created a surreal element. "It looks like drivers abandoned their vehicles. A few pushed them to the side of the road, but most of them are right where they were when the engines stopped running."

Claire added, "We've lived so long with technology I don't know if I ever knew how quiet the world could be without it."

Shelly moved closer and slipped her hand into Claire's. Bo didn't know whether she was seeking comfort or offering it. "How far do we have to walk to the nursing home?" he asked.

"Not far." Bo gave Mark another shove on the back. "Move out, oh Fearless Leader."

Mark glared at his cousin. "Why don't you walk with me?"

Bo grinned. "I thought you'd never ask. Let's go." He grabbed Mark's elbow and pulled him along, adding a cheerful whistle.

"I still think you're crazy." The words barely left Mark's mouth when the large giraffe-elephant lumbering toward them winked out, gone with the speed of an eye-blink.

Mark froze. Laughter burst from Bo. "Think about it, Mark. Where you are, magic isn't. None of these strange creatures are going to be a problem."

"Will they come back once we pass?" Mark looked stunned.

Bo shrugged. "Don't know, don't care. As long as we can pass by them without incident, I'm happy."

"Well done, Mark." Cosmos clapped Mark on the shoulder. Warm sunlight and blue skies shone from Cosmos's eyes. "Lead on."

Mark grinned at him, threw back his shoulders, and headed down the middle of Main Street. Bo walked slightly behind him, with Claire, Shelly, and Eden in the middle. Cosmos and Flicker fell in behind.

Bo glanced behind him to see the magical creatures reappear once Mark was far enough for his repel to no longer affect the mutated air.

"What is your range now, Mark?" Frank asked.

Mark shook his head and looked over his shoulder at his father. "I don't know. The first time, when I stood next to the breaker box, I had to be within three feet. But this morning Shelly had to take the mug of water into another room to turn it into coffee. I don't know if the wall between the kitchen and living room made a difference or if I'm getting stronger."

A low mechanical growling sound reached their ears.

"Halt," Cosmos yelled. "Stand still, Mark." Too late, Mark took one more step before Cosmos's words penetrated.

Ten feet in front of Mark, abandoned in the middle of the road, all four doors standing open, a black SUV roared to life. The CD player belted out a current hit, Katy Perry's Dark Horse. *There's no going back* seemed appropriate, considering the situation.

The small group huddled together and watched as the vehicle, still in gear, began a slow creep forward. As soon as it hit the perimeter of Mark's repel, the engine died and the car coasted to a halt.

Mark, white-faced and stunned, turned toward the others. "My gosh! That scared me out of a year's growth."

Bo stood next to his uncle. Matching frowns marred their faces. "Uncle Frank, are you thinking what I'm thinking?"

"If you're thinking that shouldn't have happened, then yes." He glanced down at Bo. Cosmos and Flicker came closer.

"Why are you both worried?" A frown couldn't be seen on Cosmos's face but his eyes went gray and foggy.

Frank tried to explain. "You told us that Mark is able to nullify magic. That vehicle should not have been able to start on its own."

"Are you sure, Uncle Frank?" Bo rubbed his forehead. "The car would have stopped running. The driver apparently didn't turn it off or take it out of gear. He just got out of the vehicle. Why wouldn't it have just resumed what it was doing at the moment it stopped?"

Frank shook his head, clearly puzzled. "It has to do with electricity, Cosmos. We don't have time to puzzle about it right now but soon we'll have to sit down and work out exactly what is going on with Mark." He met Cosmos's eyes.

Cosmos nodded his head in silent acknowledgment. "We'll find time soon to examine things."

Frank walked over to Mark and clapped a hand on his shoulder. "Change of plans. I'll go in front. I don't think any of the creatures will harm us. They seem to just hover in the air, clearly some child's memory of a parade. I don't think they are programmed to do anything but exist. If I'm wrong, you move in and repel them. I want to go ahead and make sure any vehicles we need to walk past are in park and the key off."

Mark nodded and stepped back, allowing his father to take lead.

Cosmos, ice replaced by the hawk's eyes, spoke up. "We need to get off the street. I can see soldiers moving our way. They must have heard the noise of the engine."

Frank nodded and led them off the street two blocks sooner than originally planned. He broke into a jog, a gait easy to maintain for long distances.

Claire fell behind. Flicker dropped back and matched her step for step.

Claire smiled at the younger woman. "Thank you. I need to get in better shape. I didn't plan on this type of activity. I'll keep up no matter what it takes. I just want my parents out of the nursing home and all of us safely back on the farm."

Bo dropped back to flank his aunt. "Don't worry, Aunt Claire. After battling Dragen and the renegades, getting Grandma and Grandpa released will be a piece of cake."

Chapter 24

"I thought you said this would be a piece of cake." Mark kept his voice low so Bo could hear him and the solider blocking the front door of the nursing home couldn't.

"Why would they be guarding a nursing home?" Bo asked. "Who does that?"

Claire leaned toward the boys. "He wasn't here yesterday. Now be quiet."

"Yes, ma'am." The boys fell silent and watched.

Frank handed a paper to the soldier. "I have permission to get my wife's parents out. We'll take responsibility for their care and get them off the premises. Surely emptying the beds here will be helpful?"

"Yes, sir." The soldier, after a quick glance at the group, turned his full attention to Frank.

"Is he ignoring Cosmos?" Bo whispered, dropping his voice even lower, not wanting to risk the wrath of his aunt.

Mark looked thoughtful. "It's like he's afraid to acknowledge Cosmos. I wonder if he's seen so many oddities that he's pretending the unexplained don't really exist."

"Shh," Claire warned the boys. They fell silent.

The soldier read through the paper, giving periodic glances at the small group. Finally, he folded the paper and handed it back to Frank. He leaned in and spoke so low Bo and Mark had to move forward a few steps to hear what he said.

"Is the little girl responsible for the man in black?"

Frank's face remained blank and uncomprehending. "What man in black?"

The soldier fell back. "That's what I was afraid of. Go on in. Good luck getting your parents out. I'm heading off duty so you're on your own. I'm not going inside for anything. My job is to keep them from coming out, and keep unauthorized people from going in. You've been given permission to get your folks out." He stepped back and carefully unlocked the door. He pulled it open and waved them through. "Good luck. You'll need it."

Cosmos moved into the middle of the group. Bo figured he was making sure the soldier didn't close the door on him.

They entered the reception area. Behind the counter the workers huddled. Each of them held an item that could double as a weapon. Bo recognized kitchen knives and an umbrella. One person held a seriously large stapler. He would have bet money it was fully loaded although he wasn't sure how much damage a staple would actually do. It looked heavy enough to hurt if used as a club. Bo recognized a combination of fear and weariness on their faces.

They relaxed when they recognized Frank and Claire. An older man, haggard and looking frail enough to be a resident, stepped forward. His badge held a photo of him looking fifteen years younger than he did today. His name was Anthony Todd, Superintendent. "Mr.Cooper. You made it back. I didn't think you would. It's not wise to have children here. It's simply too dangerous."

Frank nodded. "I understand the risks. I saw what you were up against yesterday. I've brought aid. We may be able to help minimize your difficulties before we leave."

Anthony looked hopeful. The women huddled behind him gripped their weapons and looked apprehensive. A pretty blonde stood near an open office door, looking like the least little noise would send her bolting for cover. She whispered, "Is he real? Or imaginary?"

Cosmos's eyes went soft and balmy, the color of a warm summer sky. "I'm as real as you are." He pointed at Flicker. "Flicker and I came through the rip in the sky. We know what needs to be done."

An ear-splitting scream pierced the air, coming from down the hall. Footsteps, thumps, and yells followed. Bo and Mark leaned back and looked down the hall to see two men spill through a doorway and run toward them as if the hounds of hell were on their heels.

Behind them loomed a dark figure. Mark's eyes widened in alarm. He voiced what Bo was thinking. "That thing looks like the Grim Reaper. He's not real, is he?"

Lightning flickered in Cosmos's eyes, sky-to-ground bolts lighting up his left eye. Sheet lightning flashing in the right eye. "I'm afraid this manifestation is different. Mark. Flicker. With me."

"Why me?" Mark hissed into Bo's ear. "I'm always getting shoved to the front."

"Remember Main Street." Bo pushed Mark toward Flicker and Cosmos.

"Fine." Mark's mouth thinned. "I'll help, but I'm not doing this willingly."

"You'll be fine." Cosmos gripped Mark's elbow. "Come."

Flicker actually flickered for three steps before she winked completely out to reappear behind the Reaper. Cosmos and Mark stepped apart and let the two men run past, closing the gap as soon as the men were past them.

The Reaper halted, floating in the air. Its hollow eyes surveyed Cosmos and Mark before rotating its head completely around to eye Flicker. She flicked: a moment later Bo saw her peek around a corner farther down the hallway.

"To heck with it." Bo moved fast, hoping his Uncle Frank wouldn't prevent him from helping Cosmos and Mark. He felt grim satisfaction when his uncle matched him step for step.

"What's the plan?" Bo lowered his voice hoping the nursing home staff wouldn't hear him.

Cosmos matched his tone. "I'm hoping Mark can dispel the creatures created in the minds of the elderly. I'm hoping these are creatures of the mind and have not become flesh."

"It's getting closer." Mark's voice quavered, just a bit. Bo didn't blame him. As the Reaper came closer Bo could see the awful darkness of it. A pool of ebony surrounded a body of no discernible shape; a blackness oozed toward them, reminding him of a can of spilled motor oil spreading across the concrete floor of the garage. Only, the Reaper moved through air instead of rolling on the floor.

A moment later, bright as the sun, light burst from Cosmos's eyes. To the group huddled behind them, it must have seemed like the lightning seen earlier had shot from his eyes.

"Nicely done," Bo murmured softly to his uncle. "Cosmos timed that perfectly. To the others this looks like

Cosmos destroyed the apparition. Nobody will suspect Mark did it with the light."

"Thank you." Frank reached out to pat Cosmos on the shoulder, hesitated before he made contact, and dropped his hand. Bo understood. He'd felt the touch of Cosmos's light. He wasn't anxious to find out what a man made of light actually felt like. Would it shock him? Better not to know.

"It won't stay gone," Mark reminded Cosmos. "As soon as I move out of range, it will come back."

"I know." Cosmos dimmed the light in his eyes, returning to the favored hawk eyes he'd been using. "Flicker," he called.

She stepped out of hiding, looked behind her, then scurried closer. "Cosmos, there are creatures coming out of half the rooms. They're everywhere."

He nodded. "I know. We don't pen our elderly together like this. It's a problem our Teachers and Hunters will have to deal with."

Bo went to the corner and peeked down the hallway. "Holy moly." He hurried back to stand by Mark. "It's bad." He turned to his uncle. "How did you and Aunt Claire manage yesterday?"

"We didn't." Frank looked grim. "We had to fight our way out. There was no way we could bring John and May with us and fight at the same time."

Flicker joined the group and Cosmos nodded at her. "I can put a temporary fix on the problem. I can use the nullifier. It will create a cage like we held Dragen and his followers in. This will require me leaving my own power source here. I cannot replace it until Silas returns with the Teachers and Hunters. They will have supplies and equipment with them. Leaving my controller here means I will have to rely on magic."

Cosmos hesitated. Bo could sense the worry in him. Finally, Cosmos reached down and unclipped the black box attached to his belt. He turned around and called Anthony over.

"Where is the center of this building? Would you show it to me?"

"You bet." Anthony hurried to join their small group. "I'll show you where the exact center is. You zapped that thing right out of the air. Amazing."

Cosmos nodded but didn't reply. He called to the people still huddled behind the reception desk. "Come with us. You're safer with us than you are here."

Bo ducked his head. He knew the Reaper would reappear once Mark stepped out of range. In a group, Cosmos could control the situation.

Five minutes later they stood in the center of the building. Cosmos fiddled with his device, setting it to nullify all magic within the parameters he set.

"Understand this," he said, looking at the workers. "You must not disturb this box. Don't move it. Don't touch it. As long as it functions there can be no manifestations of magic inside this building. You are here for the duration. I will return with Teachers that will help you control this situation. They will teach you how to function in this new world. Do you have enough supplies to last you for a week or so?"

Anthony nodded. "Yes, we are stocked up on medications and food. With rationing we can hang on that long.

Water is our biggest issue. It's difficult to keep patients clean and the washing machines don't function without electricity. Cleanliness is a real issue. There is a lot of waste generated that we don't know what to do with."

Cosmos nodded, his eyes going foggy and unreadable. "If you have a room that is as far from this box as its possible to get, Flicker can use her device to negate the nullifier in that room only. Bring every container you can find, and they will fill them with water. If you have laundry that needs to be cleaned, they can do that also. We can make sure you are set up to survive the next week, with care maybe ten days. I promise you Teachers will arrive soon. Then your problems will become ones of learning how to live in the new world rather than just trying to survive in the old one."

"What about Mom and Dad?" Claire sounded anxious. "Can we get them out today?"

Cosmos nodded. "Yes, we're still going to take them out. We'll give the girls three hours to generate supplies. That should be sufficient…" Cosmos stopped talking when the nullifier started beeping.

He snatched it up, turned off the alarm, and stared at the box intently. He punched a few buttons.

"Is it Hemlock?" Flicker asked.

Cosmos looked up. Bo felt his own gaze slide away. He could not meet whatever stirred in the depths of Cosmos's eyes.

"I don't know, Flicker. But the misuse of magic is on a level that makes me think it is deliberate. I only know one other person on Earth at this moment who can generate this kind of power. I believe Hemlock is nearby. I need to go after her right this minute. Bo? Mark? I want you to accompany me."

"What a minute," Frank protested. "You can't expose my boy to this kind of danger."

Mark turned red. "Dad, you still don't understand. Bo and I are destined to become Hunters. We've done this before."

"Frank…" Claire reached out and touched her husband's arm.

Frank looked undecided. "This building is safe from the creatures?"

"It is," Cosmos assured him.

"Then I'm coming too." Frank turned to his wife. "Claire, the girls are going to be busy creating supplies to get these people through the next week. You get Mom and Pop ready to leave. We'll be back as soon as we take care of this old lady Cosmos is hunting. It seems this new world is one I need to learn how to live in. I'm going."

Cosmos didn't even try to argue. He set the nullifier back on the floor and adjusted the setting. He stood up, "Flicker, you come with us to the front door. We can't get out until you create a door for us. Close it tightly after we leave. We'll capture Hemlock and Dalt and be back soon. Be ready to leave."

She nodded and smiled at Shelly and Eden. "I'll be right back."

Chapter 25

"What is this place?" Getting past the guards had been child's play. With so much misuse of magic going on, the simple 'no see' spell she had used wouldn't register on Cosmos's locator. Getting into this building Spider called 'The First National Bank of Grayson' proved even easier. Hemlock eyed the solid metal door Spider told her they must get open.

"Can you do it?" Spider pushed closer to her.

Hemlock looked at him. "Why is this room so important to you? What is behind that door that means so much to you?"

"Money." Spider's eyes shone with a crazy light. He took his eyes off the vault door long enough to look at her. "Don't you have money on your world? With what lies behind that door I can buy anything I want. I'll be rich."

Hemlock looked back at the door. She didn't see much use in money. What need did she have to buy anything when she could create it by using magic? She fingered the crude amulet bag hanging around her neck. In the bag resided the pretty purple stone she had found.

Dalt stood silent, standing apart and slightly behind Spider. He slanted a downward look at Spider. Curiosity stirred in his eyes, almost too faint to recognize. Then he looked at Hemlock, and waited, obedient to her wishes. Money didn't mean anything to him, either. Weak in the use of magic, he still possessed enough talent to take care of his needs. What more could he want?

"Can you get the vault open?" Spider pushed at Hemlock.

"Of course I can." She hobbled over to the door, placed one hand on the door, the other on her amulet bag, and pulled energy. The heavy door swung open. She stepped back, barely avoiding Spider's rush into the vault.

"Dalt," she called to the big man. He came to stand beside her, obedient as a well-trained pet.

She smiled at him. "Go into the room with Spider. Stay by his side." She added a warning: "Don't let him out of your sight."

Dalt nodded. He hesitated before stepping through the doorway.

Hemlock watched the two men. Spider touched the boxes, almost crooning to himself in anticipation. She could see tension in Dalt's body. He was no happier to be in a room with only one exit than she would be. Dalt had been useful to her. If her plans went right, she'd have no more use for him. She gripped the amulet bag with both hands, reached outward and pulled in every ounce of magic she could summon. If this didn't call Cosmos to her, nothing would.

For a moment, nothing happened. Then Dalt's eyes went wide and round. He gripped his head with both hands and an animal-like scream rent the air. Spider leaped away from the big man, stumbling in his haste. Dalt sank to his knees, agony in his eyes, and Hemlock felt a small stir of uncertainty. Surely this plan would work.

Dalt spoke. "Old woman, what have you done to me?"

"Put a few thoughts in your head, boy." She answered him in English. She'd been prepared for the change. Planned for it. "You should thank me. Stay with Spider. Do not leave this vault. Do you understand me?" The magic she had risked was illegal magic. Big magic. If this didn't draw Cosmos to them, nothing would.

She risked everything for this moment, her one chance to capture Cosmos.

Dalt rose to his feet, the expression in his eyes hard to meet. Obedience held. He nodded his acceptance to her. He'd help Spider open these boxes. He possessed magic enough for this small job.

Hemlock left them to their tasks. She needed a hiding place, one that Cosmos would not see yet close to the vault door. She'd already broken the laws of magic. What mattered a little more?

Chapter 26

Outside the nursing home, hidden from the sight of the guard on duty, Cosmos examined the locating device he held in his hand. "We need to go back to Main Street."

Mark cocked his head at Cosmos. "Can I ask you a personal question?"

Cosmos looked up, his eyes going cold and wintry. "If you must. We have to hurry to catch the old woman before she moves too far from the place she misused magic."

"You left the box with the translator inside. How can you understand and speak to us now? In English?"

The wintry chill left Cosmos's eyes, chased away by warm summer skies; his version of a smile. "I speak many languages, Mark. I have no need to break the laws of magic."

Mark grinned. "Of course you do." He turned to Bo and made a funny face. "I should have guessed that a man who can borrow moonlight and sunlight and any darn thing in the universe could also borrow language. What a gift."

Bo grinned back. "Life sure got interesting the day the sky ripped open." He narrowed his eyes at Cosmos. "I have a question, too. Do we get a tool belt when we become Hunters? Will we learn how to use those controllers?"

Mark straightened up, interest lighting his eyes. Frank stepped closer.

Cosmos nodded. "All hunters go through an apprenticeship. They are assigned to an older hunter. They travel and train with the hunter they have been paired with. Part of your training will be learning how to use the tools. When magic is the problem, we have to resort to nonmagical means to control the situation. Technology isn't restricted to the mechanized worlds."

Bo and Mark looked intrigued by Cosmos's explanation. Frank seemed reassured. "I've seen magic at work. But I've got to be honest, I don't put a lot of faith in it." He nodded toward the locator Cosmos held. "I trust technology more. I'm relieved the boys will have something to rely on rather than just thinking about a situation."

The few blocks to Main Street, without Eden and Claire slowing them down, took a few minutes.

They stood on the corner, looking up and down Main Street. Bo could tell Cosmos wanted to fly.

Cosmos gave the box he held a twist. The box split in two halves, one side smaller than the other. He turned to Frank. "You take the boys. Check out each store." He handed Frank the smaller piece. "Think of this like a pager. If you see Hemlock, press this button. It will send out a locator beam and I can come right to you."

Frank nodded. "How will I know her?"

"The boys will recognize her. They have fought with her before. She is the woman who kidnapped Eden."

Frank's mouth thinned. His eyes went cold and flat. "I get it. You go ahead. The boys and I will search the stores."

Cosmos nodded and sprang upward. Once in the air, he sped off as quickly as a beam of light leaves a flashlight when the switch is turned on.

Mark sighed. "That would be such a cool skill to have."

Bo agreed. "Let's go. Hemlock is sneaky and she's little. She could be anywhere."

Mark nodded. "I hope she's stupid enough to stay where she misused magic."

"Yeah." Bo looked in the direction Cosmos had gone, his eyes thoughtful. "But we both know Hemlock isn't stupid. I suggest we start looking in the direction Cosmos flew. Hemlock is old. She doesn't move all that fast. She might have ducked into a store between us and where Cosmos is heading."

***

Cosmos entered the First National Bank of Grayson, silent as a ghost. He didn't bother to activate the cloaking function on his device. Being dressed in black from head to toe helped him fade into the shadows. The boys, and Frank, would be kept busy. Giving them a job made them feel useful and kept them safe from the dangers Hemlock was capable of throwing at them.

He heard voices coming from behind the big metal door standing slightly ajar. He recognized Dalt's voice, but the man doing most of the talking puzzled him. Where was Hemlock?

Cosmos crept closer. He peered inside.

"Get them open. Pull them down. I want to see what is inside every drawer," the smaller man ordered. Dalt reached upward, the locked drawers no match against his magic.

A twinge of apprehension hit Cosmos at the implications. The rules of Earth were soon going to experience an upheaval of cataclysmic proportions.

Dalt saw him first. The big man's eyes widened in fear. He dropped the box he'd just removed from the wall.

The smaller man cursed and scrambled for the items spilling across the floor. "You idiot. There is jewelry in this box." He looked up at Dalt, opening his mouth to say more. The words died in his throat. He turned to see what held Dalt frozen.

"Who are you?" The smaller man rose slowly to his feet.

Dalt stuttered, "This is Cosmos." His voice dropped to a harsh whisper. "He's the Hunter looking for me and Hemlock. On my world, we call him The Executioner."

Cosmos took a step closer. Both men retreated to the back of the vault. Spider's eyes widened. A small, black object came sliding into the small vault. Behind Cosmos, the door slammed shut.

Darkness surrounded them. A low keening wail came from Dalt an eerie, strange sound to hear from such a large man.

A torrent of cursing spilled from Spider. "Dalt, shut up. Give me some light."

Cosmos's eyes glowed red in the darkness. Lava bubbled and flowed in both of them. The blinding white flared inside the vault as Cosmos pulled off the black mask hiding his face.

"I'll give you light," Cosmos said. "Judgment is here."

Chapter 27

"That's her." Bo clutched Mark's arm. "Uncle Frank, stop. We see Hemlock."

The old woman, a block ahead, had just exited a building and moved away from them.

"I don't see Dalt. I wonder where he is," Mark said.

"We need Cosmos." Nerves tickled Bo's stomach. "Page him, Uncle Frank."

They followed Hemlock from a safe distance and watched as the old woman joined a line of people standing outside the Grayson Market. She pushed into the middle, ignoring the crowd's angry muttering.

"What are we supposed to do now?" Mark stood on tiptoe and tried to look over the crowd of people.

"Why is everybody lined up here?" Bo asked his uncle.

Frank never took his eyes off the pager he held in his hand. "It's the daily allotment. Supplies are brought to town every week but it's never enough. Trucks can't get into town because the engines die as soon as they hit the contaminated area. It's the same with planes. A no-fly zone went into effect the first week after the rip. Everything has to be brought in by wagon. Only the basics make it into town. Done." Frank patted the pager before putting it in his breast pocket. "All we need now is for Cosmos to show up."

The line moved forward a few inches. Mark tried again to locate Hemlock. "I don't see her. Did she leave?"

Frank, taller than either of the boys, scanned the line ahead of him. "She's there. She's not much taller than Flicker."

"What is she doing here?" Bo asked as the line crept forward another two inches.

Frank spoke absently, keeping his eyes on the last spot he'd seen Hemlock. "She probably saw people walking away with food and decided she'd get some too. She most likely doesn't know how the distribution process works."

"Yeah, well the people on Earth don't know how magic works. That old woman is evil. I'd hate to be the one who told her 'no'," Mark muttered.

"Where is Cosmos?" Frowning, Bo's eyebrows almost met in the middle of his forehead. "He should be here by now. You have the pager going, don't you?"

"I do." Frank's lips thinned. A muscled jumped in his cheek. "Maybe one of you should go for Flicker."

Both boys shook their heads in unison.

"Won't work," Mark added. "Flicker's job is to guard Eden. She won't leave the girls. Besides, we can't get back into the nursing home, even if we could avoid the guard."

Bo's face took on a forbidding scowl, making him look older than his fourteen years. "I don't want Hemlock to see Eden. Maybe with all this magic in the air she'll forget she wants Edie."

"She might want Eden so she can disappear. The magic will follow Edie and allow Hemlock to go places she might not be able to survive in without magic." Mark opened his mouth to add more when an angry rumble of voices stopped him.

"What's going on?" Bo asked his uncle.

"Hemlock tried to push to the front of the line. Looks like she got tired of waiting. The people are so frightened of running out of food; this could turn into a lynch mob. You boys should leave before it turns violent."

"Dad." Mark's lips thinned to a hard line very similar to the one he'd just seen on his father. "Bo and I are going to be handling this type of disturbance on a regular basis. We're destined to be Hunters and believe me, the world is going to get a lot more violent before it calms down."

"We're not running, Uncle Frank. We need that old woman in custody," Bo added.

Frank looked down at the boys. "Are you willing to take down innocent people if you have to? Mobs are unthinking masses. They aren't going to care that you're boys."

Bo and Mark looked at each other, measuring and weighing Frank's words.

Mark sighed and rolled one shoulder. "We'll handle whatever we're called to handle."

Bo added, "We're going to get that old woman. Eden isn't safe as long as she runs loose."

"Then let's go and hope Cosmos shows up before we need him." Frank stepped out of line. Bo and Mark took positions on each side of him. They pushed their way closer. The nearer they got to Hemlock, the angrier the crowd became.

Screams erupted. Not angry this time, but frightened. The crowd turned to run. Frank grabbed the boys and pushed them toward the back of a stalled pickup truck.

"Get into the bed," he shouted over the noise of the crowd. Bo and Mark scrambled over the tailgate.

Frank followed. They crouched, watching as the crowd scattered.

Bo shuddered. He hadn't known, before this minute that panic created such a pulsing energy of fear he could feel deep in his bones. He half-rose to peek over the top of the cab. Mark popped up beside him.

"Do you see her?" Mark whispered.

Frank rose up on Bo's left side. As he stood in a half-crouch he patted the pocket holding the pager, checking to make sure it was still there.

"There she is," Bo whispered.

"What's she doing?" Mark looked as puzzled as he sounded.

Frank's voice went low and angry. "She's establishing her dominance. She's using lightning. We've seen oddities ever since the sky ripped." Frank's voice went even grimmer. "But we haven't yet seen somebody control it."

Bo raised up on tiptoe. "Wow, she's using lightning like javelins. Throwing them at people. When she hits somebody, they go down like bowling pins." He sounded awed.

"At least she's not killing anybody yet." Mark sounded thoughtful. The pupils in his eyes shrank, making the blue of his eyes stand out. He looked surprisingly dangerous.

One corner of Bo's mouth curved upward. "You know what this means, don't you?" he asked Mark.

"What?" Suspicion warred with wariness on Mark's face. He knew Bo too well.

Frank sighed. "Bo's right, Mark. Let's go."

"Right? What's right? What do you two know that I don't?" A red flush spread over Mark's cheeks.

Frank and Bo jumped to the street, keeping the truck between them and Hemlock.

"Hey." Mark leaped over the side of the truck. "Wait for me."

"Looks like she's going into the store," Frank observed.

"Does she know what guns are?" Mark took a few running steps to catch up with his father and Bo. "I don't see the soldiers being very patient with her even if she is old."

A loud volley of shots rang out, followed by glass shattering. The windows facing the street disintegrated. Before the last piece of glass hit the pavement, guns came flying through the window to land in a pile on the sidewalk.

"That answers that question." Frank looked thoughtful. "I'm glad we weren't standing in front of the building."

"Yeah," Bo agreed. "It makes the next part of our capture easier. No guns in the store. At least, no guns in the hands of the soldiers."

"Just one mean old woman." Mark rubbed the back of his neck. Then Bo's words hit him. "What do you mean, capture?"

Bo patted Mark on the back, then gave him a sharp shove. "Go for it, Mark. Charge."

Mark stumbled forward. Before he could catch his balance, Bo and Frank hustled him forward.

"Hurry, Mark. Get into range before the old witch realizes what you can do."

Mark protested. "Why can't we just wait for Cosmos? This is his job."

Bo grabbed his arm. "Because Cosmos should have been here by now. We can't risk losing Hemlock."

They stepped inside the store. Bo saw bodies lying around the room. Whether they were dead, or alive, he couldn't tell. Two soldiers were pinned halfway up the wall. How, or by what, Bo didn't know. Arms and legs were splayed wide. He half expected to see spikes hammered through their hands and feet. Their angry eyes and creative cursing made it plain they were very much alive.

"I want my share." The old woman looked around the store.

"Why?" Mark looked puzzled, then horrified when Hemlock turned to look at him.

Bo nudged Mark forward. "Get a little closer, Mark, so she can hear you better."

Mark turned and glared at him. "Will you quit pushing me?"

Frank patted Mark on the shoulder, then added his own nudge, sending Mark forward a few more steps. "Go ahead, son. It's bad manners to shout."

"You, too?" Mark turned and glared at his father.

Frank smiled. "Remember Main Street, Mark. Remember Main."

"Oh." A big grin spread across Mark's face. "All right, then."

He turned toward Hemlock and launched himself at her. She grabbed the bag hanging around her neck, a look of intense concentration on her face, followed by concern. Then Mark was on her.

She struggled but her frail body couldn't stand against one adult man and two determined boys.

Bo removed the necklace from Hemlock. They had to lift and carry her to keep her close to Mark. She refused to walk on her own. Mark walked over to the back wall until his ability to nullify magic took effect and the men fell from the wall.

The older man stood up and shook himself. "Thanks. We had no idea a person could control whatever came through the rip in the sky." He straightened his clothes.

The younger man, blond hair cropped short in a military buzz, went outside to retrieve their weapons.

The remaining soldier held his hand out. He shook Frank's hand and ignored the boys. "Sir, how did you break the hold the woman had on us?"

Frank looked uneasy. Bo knew he was struggling with what to tell and what he should hold back. Mark's safety depended on what his uncle said next.

Frank cleared his throat. His eyes landed on the necklace Bo still held. He reached over and took it. He held it high, showing it to the soldier. "I believe this holds power. The old woman had her hand wrapped around it when we tackled her. My nephew got it off her, and the magic, or whatever you call it, stopped."

"We'll take charge of that, sir." The first soldier didn't give Frank time to argue. He plucked it from Frank's hand.

Behind them, the blond-haired soldier spoke up. "We'll take charge of the prisoner. Leave us your name and address. We'll want to question you in depth later."

Bo and Mark started to protest. Frank raised a hand and hushed them before they could speak.

"She's a danger to everybody around her," Frank warned them. "Her name is Hemlock. She looks old and weak but I would advise you to keep her feet and hands bound. Tape her mouth if you must but whatever you do, don't leave her unattended."

"We know our job, sir." The older man glared.

He ignored Mark's whispered words, "Yeah, we weren't the ones glued to a wall." He did send the boy an unfriendly glare before turning back to Frank.

"Your job is done, sir. Take your bag of allotted goods and go home. Someone will stop by later for your statements."

"Yes, sir." Frank grabbed each boy by the elbow and dragged them out of the store. They hurried down the street before stopping to catch their breath.

Mark burst out, "Are you crazy, Dad? Hemlock will be loose before those men catch their breath."

"Think about it, Mark." Frank's face turned stony. A muscle in his jaw tensed. "Nobody can know what you are capable of. We caught Hemlock because she couldn't use magic when you're nearby. Those men fell off the wall because of you. If they find out you can nullify the effects of magic, every military faction on the face of the Earth will be after you."

Mark swallowed hard. Bo rubbed his forehead, his movements jerky and quick.

"What should we do?" A shattered, vulnerable look crossed Mark's face.

Frank squeezed Mark's shoulder, comforting, giving strength. "We find Cosmos and we find him fast. Right now, we know where Hemlock is. In about fifteen minutes I think she'll be gone again."

"Right," Bo nodded. "Let's find Cosmos."

Chapter 28

"Dad, somebody needs to follow the soldiers and Hemlock. Bo can do it, I can do it, or you can. But somebody needs to keep eyes on that old woman."

Bo could tell his uncle wanted to curse, tension pouring from him. He could see it in Frank's tight jaw, his grim mouth, and angry eyes. Uncle Frank didn't want to leave the boys but he recognized the truth in Mark's words.

"All right!" Frank snapped, each word he spoke clipped and terse. "I don't want either of you boys alone, so I'll follow Hemlock. I've got the pager. When I know where she's at I'll make sure it's still activated so Cosmos can find me."

"You boys find Cosmos. If you can't locate him in ten minutes promise me you'll go for Flicker and let her take over. She's trained for this kind of work."

Mark and Bo nodded their agreement. They could feel the minutes ticking. The longer they talked the further away Hemlock got.

"Go, Dad. They're already out of sight. Go find them."

Frank nodded and pulled Mark into a hard, fast hug. He clapped Bo on the shoulder and jogged off in the direction he'd last seen Hemlock

The boys hurried down the street to the building they'd first seen Hemlock come out of.

"Didn't Cosmos go in here?" Mark sounded puzzled. "How could he have missed her? Where could he be?"

"Something has gone wrong." Bo frowned.

"Yeah," Mark sounded thoughtful. "I still wish I knew where Dalt was."

"Maybe Cosmos and Dalt got into it and Hemlock made a break for it while they fought?"

"We could *maybe* all day," Mark said. "But we need to figure out what to do."

Bo shook his head, still puzzled. "It's hard to picture Cosmos needing help. Dalt is really big, but if Cosmos turns the light on him, he's done for. Nobody escapes the effects of the Light of Truth."

I should know, he thought. He'd felt the light when Cosmos judged Eden. A shudder of horror moved through him at the memory. He'd only caught a small portion of the light and the experience would never leave him. The light had changed Eden. She was no longer a carefree little girl. She considered every move she made, terrified she'd make a mistake. Her childhood was forever changed.

Mark glanced upward at the big sign above the doorway. "This is the bank. What would Hemlock want in a bank?"

"We won't know standing outside." Bo pushed Mark toward the doorway.

Mark turned to glare at his cousin. "I really wish you'd stop pushing me to the head of the line. Did it ever occur to you I might want to walk behind?"

Bo grinned. "Sure, but I'm braver when you go first."

Mark grunted, shook his head, and gave up. He pushed open the door and walked into the bank.

Bo followed to stand at his shoulder. "There's nobody here. Where in the world did Cosmos go?" Silence. Bo turned to look at Mark and saw him staring at the locked vault.

"You don't think…?" Bo started.

"I do." Mark stopped him. "It's the only answer. Somehow the old woman trapped Cosmos in the one place in Grayson light can't get out of."

"You think Cosmos is in the vault?" The idea stunned Bo almost into speechlessness.

"Not just Cosmos, but Dalt too."

"How do we find out?" Bo asked. "How are we supposed to get the vault open?"

Mark shrugged. "I want to know what happens if we do get it open. Do you think Cosmos is going to be reasonable? Or will he blast everybody in sight?"

"I hadn't thought of that." A thoughtful expression settled on Bo's face, gradually changing into fear. "I've seen what Cosmos can do when he's in control. Do you think he's angry?"

A bellow answered him. From inside the vault, Cosmos yelled, "Get me out of here!"

"That answers that question," Mark muttered. "How in the world can he yell loud enough to be heard through that thick metal door?"

"Better question," Bo responded. "How can he hear us?"

Another yell answered him. "Do you think I only borrow with my eyes? I borrow with my ears, too. Nothing is secret from me if I'm listening. Stop talking and get this door open."

"I'm not kidding." Mark sounded anxious. "I don't know how we're supposed to unlock that door. We're not bank robbers. Opening locks isn't one of my skills."

"Mine either but we'd better come up with something." Bo rubbed his head. He called out to Cosmos, "Can you use magic?"

Cosmos responded in a language neither boy had ever heard. Bo was pretty sure the translation would be unfit for their ears. They sounded rude to him.

Finally, Cosmos calmed down enough to revert back to English. "Hemlock slid a nullifier into the room. I don't know where she got it, or how she learned to work it. It might very well be the one they used to escape from the prison we had them in before they entered this world. I can't use magic in here. You should be able to use magic out there. Bo, send Mark outside and you try to open the door."

"I'm no good at magic," Bo protested. "You need Shelly here, or Eden. Flicker could do this in a heartbeat."

"Just do it!" Cosmos yelled, then lapsed back into words neither boy could understand.

"I wonder who judges the judge." Mark frowned at the vault door. "I don't think Cosmos is acting very professional."

"He hears everything you're saying, you know." Bo shoved Mark toward the front door. "Are you willing to risk his light touching you when he gets out of there? And he will get out, make no mistake about that."

"Yeah, yeah. Light burns. I get that. I saw what he did when the convicts broke into the house when we first found I nullify magic. Believe me, judgment is preferable to purification"

"Don't be so sure of that." Bo opened the door, stepping to the side so Mark could exit. "Dying is feeling nothing. Living means having to suffer and remember every minute of every day. If the pain is deep enough, purification might be a kindness."

Mark looked thoughtful. "I hadn't thought of that but living also means having the opportunity to put things right. I'd hate having choices taken from me."

Another roar from the vault halted their conversation. Mark scampered through the door to the sidewalk. Bo walked back to the vault. He didn't have a clue how to unlock a door as secure as this one.

Ten minutes later, sweat dripping down his face, his last shred of patience vanished. Bo yelled, "Shut up, Cosmos. You've given me every piece of advice you can think of. You're not helping."

"What can be so hard about opening a door? You will it open!" Cosmos roared back.

"Well, yeah," Bo muttered. "There's the problem. I'm not sure, deep down, I really want you out. You seem to be a tad out of control."

Silence, more frightening than Cosmos's curses, assaulted Bo's senses. He stood up, carefully brushed off his knees and began a careful creep toward freedom.

Soft, silky, smooth as butter, Cosmos spoke, sounding as if he stood at Bo's shoulder. "You're not thinking of leaving me here, are you, Bo?"

The front door opened and Mark entered. Sensitive to the atmosphere, he whispered, "What's going on? Are you giving up?"

A loud thump rattled the vault door. "Of course not," Bo spoke, words tumbling over each other as he tried to calm Cosmos. "I'd never stop trying but I can't get the door unlocked. We need a Plan B."

"Plan B had better not involve leaving me here." The calmness in Cosmos's voice was not reassuring.

"He's not taking this well, is he?" Mark commented.

"You think?" Bo frowned, ideas running through his head like a hamster on a wheel. Panic tended to throw his brain into overdrive, a feeling he was becoming all too familiar with.

He sighed. "Cosmos, you said you can borrow from other places. Are you familiar with a laser?"

More silence. An odd note in Cosmos's voice brought grins to Mark's and Bo's faces, expressions they hastily wiped clear lest Cosmos be looking. How could one tell about the strange properties of Cosmos's eyes?

"I am." Cosmos finally spoke. "Please move away from the door."

"No problem," Mark murmured. He opened the door to the street and they left the building. Bo tread so close behind him he almost stepped on Mark's heels. They crouched behind a post office drop-box. It didn't give them a lot of protection but it was metal, and sturdy.

A few moments later, a flash of light lit up the air.

"Sort of reminds me of what I think a nuclear flare would look like." Bo spoke softly, knowing no amount of whisper would hide him from Cosmos if Cosmos chose to listen.

"He's out." Mark drew into a tighter ball. "Whether that's a good thing or not, I don't have a clue."

Above them, in a cool, controlled tone, Cosmos spoke. "Are you going to hide here all day? Or shall we go catch a wicked, old woman?"

Chapter 29

Bo and Mark rose to their feet. Bo cocked his head and gave Cosmos a long, measuring look. "How long are your eyes going to be red?"

Mark took a half-step slide to the left, distancing himself from Bo and readying himself to dive behind the drop-box if it proved necessary.

Even behind the black cloth, they could see the shape of Cosmos's mouth go thin and tight. "The state of my eyes will last until my mood changes. Right now," he stopped speaking and the red flow of lava in his eyes erupted, before subsiding to bubbles and burps.

Bo shrugged. "Okay, but I'm walking behind you at all times until you calm down."

"Understood." Cosmos turned. "Come, we'll retrieve Dalt, then go after the old woman. I take it the pager beeping means Frank has her under surveillance?"

Mark ran a few steps to catch up to Bo. "Dalt is still alive?"

Cosmos stopped, hand on the door to the bank. He slowly swiveled his head and stared at the boys. For one short moment, his eyes went completely black, before the lava returned. "I judge. At times, I execute. I do not murder. Follow me, and see for yourself."

Mark whispered into Bo's ear. "I didn't think I'd ever be glad to see the lava but the red is better than the black."

"I can hear you." Cosmos's voice sounded next to them, even though the man himself was pulling open the vault door. "Hurry, we don't have all day and I suspect Dalt would feel better if he could see you."

The boys ran to catch up, sliding to a halt at the door of the vault. Neither one felt inclined to enter the place where Cosmos had been trapped.

Cosmos released enough light from his eyes to light up the vault. Dalt huddled in the far corner. Shock ran through Bo at the sight of the big man sitting huddled on the floor. The Dalt he knew had been frightening. Tall, broad, with unreadable eyes that seemed devoid of all human emotions.

"He's not so scary now," Bo said softly to Mark. Pity moved in him at the utter dejection in the big man's posture.

Dalt raised his head, looking at them with eyes that reminded Bo of a stray dog he'd once seen one that had been beaten so cruelly, he'd lost the use of one leg.

Mark poked his head forward and surveyed the vault's interior. "Where's the other man?

"Spider?" Dalt's voice sounded odd. Hesitant, and thin, he curled into himself, managing to make himself look smaller by half. "Spider wouldn't stop screaming. I closed my eyes so I wouldn't have to see him. When I opened my eyes, Spider was gone."

Cosmos stiffened. "Nothing hides from the Truth. This man, Spider, judged himself. I did not purify until he chose."

Mark hastened to reassure. "Nobody is saying you acted hastily."

Cosmos swung his head to glare at Mark, his eyes for one split second going icy and glacial rather than the red of molten lava.

Mark added, "I'm really grateful I don't have to see a dead body. Purification seems to be a neat, tidy clean-up."

"It is our way," Cosmos finally said. "Magic was never meant to be part of a mechanized world. To be honest, we never thought it could happen. Dragen has a lot to answer for. Teachers will come and your people will need to adapt or die. Magic is a harsh reality. Learn to live with it or it will make its own rules."

The pager on his belt beeped again, reminding them of Frank's need. "Come." Cosmos spoke to Dalt. "I need for you to come with us. Stay by my side. Follow my orders."

The big man rose to his feet. "I seem to do nothing but follow orders." Bitterness colored his words. "I was happier before you judged me. I thought following orders was all I had to do to be good. Finding out everything I did wrong hurts. All I feel now is pain."

Cosmos spoke gently to Dalt. "Doing the wrong thing should hurt. But without the knowledge of right and wrong how would you be able to choose to do right?"

Dalt sighed and said nothing. He fell into step behind Cosmos. The small group left the building. Mark took time to push the vault door shut but nothing could block the hole from Cosmos's laser beam.

"Aren't you going after Hemlock?" Mark ran a few steps to catch up with Cosmos. Bo stayed three steps behind. He'd felt the light of justice that Cosmos was made from. *Once was enough, thank you very much.*

Cosmos swiveled his head around to look down at Mark. Bo took two steps to his left, then paused when a strange thought floated through his mind. Would his light even work on Mark? Ephemeral and fleeting, afraid Cosmos might catch it, Bo let the thought slide away.

"I will retrieve Hemlock. But first, we need to get Flicker and the girls back to the farm. We need Eden as far away from the old woman as possible. Hemlock is without Dalt, now. She'll need somebody to help her. Eden is still young enough to be corrupted. She will want Eden now more than ever."

Mark dropped back to walk with Bo. His face betrayed his worry. "I feel worse now than I did before."

Bo nodded. "I know. We told the soldiers to keep Hemlock tied, hands and feet, but I don't think they can hold her. Not here, in Grayson, where the air is already saturated with magic."

Dalt, stoic and silent up until now, nodded his head. When he spoke, his voice was steady and mild. "You are right. The old woman will be free when she chooses. Inside the dark room, before she closed us in, she used great magic to give us the gift of your language. She talks like you do now." His head dipped lower, his voice saddened. "As do I. I have thoughts in my head now I never had before. I think she did something to my head besides give me language. I don't think she meant to change how I think, but she did. I did not break this law of magic. Hemlock did, but I bear the burden of it."

The boys looked at him. Curious, Bo asked, "How did you survive the judgment?"

Dalt shook his head, refusing to answer. Bo sympathized. He didn't like to talk about the Light of Truth, either.

Cosmos answered. "I do not pass judgment. The individual chooses. Dalt chose to atone."

"How will he do that?" Mark asked.

Cosmos didn't speak, increasing his pace to a slow jog. The others followed.

Dalt said, "I chose to protect the little one. I will give my life to keep your Eden safe."

His words stunned the boys. They froze in their tracks, mouths hanging open, before breaking into a hard run to catch up.

Bo sprinted forward to run beside Cosmos, forgetting his vow to stay behind him at all times.

"Are you crazy, Cosmos? My sister? You're risking Eden to give Dalt redemption?"

Cosmos turned his fiery eyes onto the boy. Bo held his ground, waiting for Cosmos's answer.

"I risk nothing," the man finally said. "You know where the light touches, truth is revealed. I know Dalt, everything about him from the moment of his conception to this place in time. He is not guilty, like Hemlock is. He did nothing with evil intent. He simply followed orders from the person he owed allegiance to." Cosmos's eyes lightened, going from molten lava to something softer. "He is a simple man, Bo, unable to make decisions. He follows orders. He gives blind obedience. He makes no choices of his own except this one. He wants to make right what he did wrong. Everybody deserves a chance to make things right."

Bo pinched his lips tight on the words he longed to say. He gave a single nod to Cosmos and dropped back to match steps with Mark." I just wish he wasn't using my sister to make things right."

Mark managed a shoulder shrug without breaking stride. "You never know, Bo. Dalt might be just the protection Eden will need. It's a cinch the old woman will think Dalt hers. He might be the very element of surprise Eden will need."

They fell silent, conserving their breath until they arrived at the nursing home. The guard had left his post and the front door stood open. On entering the reception area they found Flicker and the girls helping their grandmother put on a sweater. The old woman gave them a sweet smile. She patted Mark on the cheek. "Aren't you a lovely young man? Thank you so much for coming to see me."

Her faded blue eyes shone with pleasure but no recognition. She smiled at Bo. "I don't remember you. Should I?"

His heart ached a little bit. He remembered milk and homemade cookies, and lots of laughter. "Hi, Grandma. I remember you. That's good enough." He leaned forward and kissed her wrinkled cheek.

She beamed at him. "I'm so glad you do." Then she looked at Claire. For a moment her eyes sharpened. "Claire, when did you get here?"

Claire blinked her eyes to clear them, her voice husky. "I just got here, Mama. We're taking you home."

"Home?" the woman blinked. "To the farm?"

"Yes, Mama." Claire buttoned the last button on May's sweater. "We're going home to the farm."

"Is John coming? I won't leave him, you know." May's hands fluttered, patting her hair, her clothes, and Claire. Her restless hands betrayed her anxiety.

"Papa is coming too," Claire reassured her mother. "Look, he's in his wheelchair. We're taking him home with us."

A bright, warm smile of pleasure lit May's face. "That's good. As long as we can take Papa, I'm ready."

Mark stepped behind the wheelchair but Dalt stopped him. He put a gentle hand on Mark's shoulder. "Let me push the chair. I'm bigger and stronger than you are." He spoke simply, stating a fact.

Mark looked at Dalt, seeing his quiet face, his soft brown eyes. He nodded and let go of the handles on the chair. "Thank you, Dalt. I appreciate the help."

Dalt looked surprised; an uncertain smile tilted his lips upwards. "I don't believe anybody ever said 'thank you' to me before." His smile widened. "I think I like it."

Cosmos and Flicker had their heads together, talking. Finally Cosmos gave a sharp head nod. He walked over to the group of nursing home personnel. "We're expecting a group of Teachers and Hunters to arrive soon. When they get here, I would like to base them here. You have adequate housing facilities and they can help keep the elderly from manifesting dangerous entities."

Anthony nodded, relief evident on his face. "I agree to your terms. We'll house your workers and help them in any way we can. We certainly need help if we're to care for the residents properly. We can't go back to the way it was. Nobody was being adequately cared for. We had to make rounds in groups just to get daily medication to the residents. We'd be grateful for any help and training your people can give us."

Goodbyes and thanks said, Cosmos urged his small group out the front door. John's wheelchair didn't seem to tax Dalt's strength. He pushed the chair with ease. The old man sat hunched over, chin on his chest, oblivious to all.

Chapter 30

They stood on Main Street. It was littered by abandoned vehicles as far as they could see. The crazy parade of impossible animals and bobbing balloon figures still careened crazily from curb to curb.

"This feels so eerie." Claire spoke softly. She held May's elbow to prevent her wandering away. "Usually, by this time of day, we see representatives of each family moving about collecting their daily allotments."

"How are we going to get out of here? We can't take John and May out using the secret path. The wheelchair would never get through the fence, let alone the brush and uneven terrain." Frank looked at Cosmos.

The molten lava left Cosmos's eyes, replaced by a gray, misty fog. "These vehicles will work as long as Mark is in one?" he asked Frank.

Frank nodded. "I believe so, yes. But we don't have a hope of getting past the guards. Nobody has been allowed to leave town for weeks. They're trying to contain the contamination. They don't know yet that the air itself is the problem."

"Time is a factor," Cosmos replied. "I can't take time to take charge of Hemlock until I know Eden is safe. If we had more time, Flicker and I could take you all out, one at a time, and the guards would never see us. Harley is waiting near the clearing with the horses and the wagon.

He's probably starting to worry about us. Hemlock being here has changed the game. I need to get to her before she disappears." The gray fog in Cosmos's eyes took on a dull, ominous red before returning to gray. "I can't take time to transport you to the clearing. So our best means of escape is a vehicle. I suggest you choose one that everybody can fit in.

"Frank, you'll drive. Claire, you stay with your mother. Dalt? I'm putting you in charge of John. Keep him safe and make sure you stay with the group."

Dalt nodded. Bo felt a strange shift in his feelings toward the big man. Looking at Dalt, he believed the man would die protecting his grandfather, even against Hemlock.

Cosmos added, "Flicker, your job remains the same. Keep Eden safe. Shelly, you help her. Mark..." He tilted his head and surveyed the boy. "Your job is simple. Stay with the vehicle. It won't run if you aren't within range of the engine."

Cosmos turned his attention to the group. "Get clear of the town. As soon as you lose sight of the town, pull over and abandon the vehicle. Harley will be waiting near the clearing. Explain what has happened then load May and John into the wagon and head for the farm. I'll catch up once I make sure everything is taken care of here."

Mark frowned. "Why can't we just drive the truck home?"

"Mark!" Claire sounded shocked. "Borrowing a vehicle is one thing. I won't condone stealing it."

Mark winced. "I guess I didn't think, Mom. I'm sorry."

Cosmos turned, waving a hand at Bo. "Bo, you come with me."

Claire squeaked. She grabbed Bo and gave him a big hug. Then she ran to catch her mother. A colorful balloon floating at eye level had caught her attention. Claire grabbed hold of her elbow and gently steered her back to the group.

Flicker gave Bo a stern look. "Remember your training."

He nodded at her.

Cosmos gave him no more time to say anything. He started walking down the street. Bo ran to catch up with him.

"What's the plan?" he asked.

"We're going to get Hemlock. That means we have to either convince the guards to turn her over to us, or incapacitate the guards."

"You're not going to kill them, are you?" An anxious twinge twisted Bo's stomach.

Cosmos looked down, little fountains of lava spurting upwards in his eyes, a nice change from the angry red and foggy gray Bo had seen far too much of. "I really wish I knew why you persist in thinking of me as a harmful entity. I don't kill people."

He turned away, but not before Bo heard him murmur, "I don't have to."

They approached the check-in post. Cosmos slowed his steps. "Standing behind me won't protect you, Bo. I'm a being of light. Everything goes through me."

Bo sighed and stepped back to Cosmos's side. "Give me a break, Cos. I'm only a Hunter-in-training. I don't have a clue what to do."

"Just follow your instincts. Right now, I don't anticipate doing anything more than talking."

"Halt." The guard stepped in front of them. Bo recognized the soldier as the younger of the two men he'd recently seen glued to a wall.

"I know you." The soldier lowered his weapon. Just as the guard outside the nursing home had done, he ignored Cosmos. "You apprehended the crazy lady and rescued us from an embarrassing situation."

"Where is Hemlock now?" Cosmos responded. "She's a criminal from my world and needs to be placed in protective custody."

"We've got the situation under control." Blondie--Bo couldn't think of anything else to call him, the name on his shirt was certainly unpronounceable--stiffened.

"You don't understand the danger," Cosmos tried to explain. "The air that came through the rip in the sky has contaminated your Earth. As long as Hemlock has access to the magic, she is dangerous."

Blondie stiffened even more and half raised his weapon.

"We're not crazy," Bo protested. "Cosmos, show him some magic."

"I'd rather not." Cosmos glanced down at Bo. A brief scatter of something glittery and light danced in his eyes for a moment. "He seems a bit jumpy."

"Look--" Bo barely stopped himself from calling the man Blondie. "We know what has happened, how, and why. Hemlock really can control magic. If you don't believe that, she will escape and you guys will look really stupid."

Behind them, Bo heard an engine fire up. He locked gazes with Cosmos. Time was running out. Blondie heard the engine, too. He turned toward the guardhouse, waving his arms and yelling.

Soldiers came running. Cosmos tried again. "I need to know where you're holding the old woman. She needs to be immobilized so she can't access magic."

Blondie ignored him. Behind them Bo heard the truck coming closer. Not just the truck, he realized, but underneath the sound of the motor he heard voices shouting and screaming. He hoped the screams weren't from his group. Cosmos grabbed his arm and pulled him behind the guard shack.

"Stay here. Don't move," Cosmos ordered. Bo nodded, waited until Cosmos left, and then moved until he could see around the corner of the shack.

"Every soldier in town must be here." He didn't realize he'd spoken out loud until he heard the sound of his own voice. "How in the world is Uncle Frank going to get through that crowd?

Bo counted a dozen soldiers. Some held weapons on the approaching truck. Behind the truck, people emerged from inside the buildings. Bo couldn't begin to count them all but it looked like the citizens of Grayson outnumbered the soldiers three to one. A couple of men got close enough to the bed of the pick-up truck and tried to haul themselves up. Bo could see Dalt and Mark pounding on hands and pushing people off.

Nobody paid him any attention so he stepped out to get a clearer view. Uncle Frank lay on the horn, trying to warn people to get out of his way. The soldiers weren't budging. "I hope they don't start shooting at the truck."

Flicker flicked and reappeared behind the soldiers. She waved her hands in the air. The soldiers yelled, and dropped their weapons. The gun barrels gleamed a dull red in the sunlight. The composite material of the stocks melted. Seriously hot, Bo decided.

Movement above caught his eyes and he looked upward. Cosmos hung in the air, searching for Hemlock. The old woman was Cosmos's primary concern.

Bo stepped away from the guard house, looking toward the building closest to it. "I see her. Flicker," he called to her. She still stood behind the line of soldiers, and was closest to him. "Come and help me."

She ran to him and Bo pointed to two burly soldiers carrying the old woman, still bound hands and feet, between them. They moved away from the mob on Main Street, taking her around the corner of a building half a block away.

"Flicker, they're going to take her away. We need to get her now."

"Cosmos sees her," Flicker reassured Bo. "I can't get to her from here."

Bo gaped at her. "You can teleport. How can you not get to her?"

Flicker shook her head. "I don't flick when I choose it. I flick when I'm in danger. I can't control the ability, Bo. I only react to it. My job is to clear a path for the truck. If you want to help, go to the back of the guard shack and get to the side of the road in case Cosmos needs you to help with the guards."

She turned and ran back toward the slowly moving truck. Bo slipped back behind the shack. Before he could dash across the road to the building a roar of sound reached him.

A second group of people came running down Main Street. So many people filled the street Bo couldn't see. He looked around for something to stand on. His eyes landed on metal barrels outside the guard shack. In one lithe move, he clambered on them. From the top of the barrel it was an easy pull to climb to the roof of the shack. He stood up. From this height he saw the length of the street.

Closest to him stood the unarmed guards. Next was the truck. Bo gave his uncle full credit for keeping the truck moving, inch by inch toward freedom. The citizens of Grayson surged toward the truck. Mark and Dalt pushed people away, but as fast as they'd get one person off another tried to climb on.

Through the windshield he could see Shelly's frightened face. Eden must have been on the floor. He couldn't see her at all.

Farther down Main Street, Bo saw a group of people that struck fear into his heart. The citizens were just frightened people. Good and honest for the most part. The group moving toward the truck wore orange jumpsuits. Even from this distance, Bo felt the danger.

"Cosmos!" No response. Bo turned to look at the building Cosmos had gone into. Bo lay down on his stomach, and slid off the roof to hang suspended before dropping to the ground.

Cosmos appeared. The red lava was back in his eyes. If Bo had had time he'd have been interested in timing how close together the eruptions in Cosmos's eyes were.

Bo couldn't begin to tell Cosmos what he'd seen. Words clogged his throat. He raised his arm and pointed.

Cosmos floated upward. Right before he took off Bo managed to yell, "Where's Hemlock?"

Cosmos hovered. "Gone. By the time I got to them, the soldiers were down, and she was gone." He looked at the milling crowd. "My guess is she will join the newcomers, the ones who look the most dangerous." Cosmos gained altitude and called down, "To arms, Bo! Use those weapons you were given. Try the slingshot first. You can maintain some distance using it."

"Good idea." Bo pulled Ian's slingshot out of his back pocket. He opened the bag holding the nicely rounded stones.

He ran, giving the soldiers berth, moving until he could get some of the orange jumpsuits in his sight. "Sweet," he crooned when the first stone flew straight and true to the head of a particularly scary man. He dropped, out cold.

Four stones later, Bo figured out the bag holding the stones must be imbued with magic. *Ian*, he thought, *you are one clever boy.* The bag remained full no matter how many stones he pulled out.

"Uh, oh." Panic set his stomach on fire. Three of the group he'd labeled 'Bad Guys' had finally located him as the culprit laying them out. They peeled away from the main group to come at him.

He ran toward the soldiers. Maybe the bad guys wouldn't follow him if he was surrounded by the good guys.

***

"This didn't go as planned," Bo muttered. He scrambled to his feet, afraid if he sat much longer he'd get run over. Whether by the truck his uncle drove, or the crowd milling around.

"Stop hitting me!" he yelled at the soldier who had struck him earlier. "I'm on your side." The soldier let fly another punch. Bo dodged, and decided it would be safer helping Dalt and Mark keep people from climbing into the truck.

"Get in!" Mark yelled at him. "Get up here and use the sling shot from here. You can keep the jumpsuits from getting too close to us."

Bo held his arm up and Dalt reached down and grabbed him, hauling him into the bed of the pickup. Bo stepped around his grandfather in the wheelchair and took up a position close by the tailgate. At this height he could shoot over the heads of the citizens and aim at the jumpsuits.

Dalt and Mark continued to push, shove, and beat people to prevent them from climbing onto the slow-moving truck.

Claire did her best to keep her mother from crawling out of the truck, while making sure her father didn't tip over in his chair.

"Eden!" Shelly's scream caught Bo's attention. He let fly another stone before scrambling to the front of the pick-up bed to see what had Shelly so upset.

Eden crawled out the truck window and, with the same agility she used when getting on the pony, scrambled upward onto the roof of the vehicle. Frank braked. The truck stopped its forward crawl.

Cosmos, using his ability to project his voice, yelled, "Close your eyes!"

Bo squeezed his eyes shut. Even behind closed lids he saw a bright flash of light followed by a sonic boom. Between the light and the sound, Bo wondered if he'd ever hear or see normally again.

Cosmos let out a roar of anger.

"Oh, geez," Mark groaned. "I think Cosmos is angry again."

"You think?" Bo scrambled to stand beside Mark. "I don't think he's stopped being angry since Hemlock locked him in the vault."

The mob was dazed and disorganized. Cosmos flew higher in the sky, circling, searching.

He gave another roar and swooped, moving so fast Bo couldn't follow his descent. "He really can move with the speed of light when he wants to."

Mark nodded in agreement. "I think he's caught Hemlock. Look."

Cosmos rose into the air, Hemlock dangling in his arms. The boys yelled in their excitement.

"She's unconscious." Mark punched Bo on the arm. "Cosmos's flash bomb must have knocked her out."

The boys waved at Cosmos. He spoke to them, using his ability to throw his voice where he willed it. "I'm going ahead to the clearing. I'll brief Harley, then be back."

Before the boys could finish nodding, Cosmos and Hemlock were gone.

"Eden, get back in the truck!" Shelly begged.

The boys turned around to see Eden had crawled on top of the cab. She stood up straight, her face set in a mutinous scowl, the kind of expression that turned Bo's stomach into a hard ball of dread.

Behind him, Mark yelled, "Bo, they're coming again! The orange jumpsuits. They're on their feet and heading this way. They look really mad!"

Bo looked over his shoulder. The group he most feared were standing up, even the ones he'd knocked out with rocks from the slingshot. He didn't give himself much of a chance if they laid hands on him.

He turned back to Eden and reached for her.

She backed away from him, getting so close to the front of the truck he feared she'd go sliding onto the hood.

Frank opened the door and stepped onto the running board. He reached for his niece. "Edie, get in. I can't drive with you standing up here."

"No. Mama told me I have to do the right thing. If there is a fight, I'm supposed to fight." Tears flooded her eyes and her hair, always full of static electricity, floated around her head.

She pointed at the group in orange jumpsuits. "Those are bad people."

She pointed at the citizens. "Those people are scared."

She turned around and pointed at the soldiers. "Those people are wrong."

She turned back to Bo. "I want this over. I want to go home. I want all of this to stop."

Her tears fell harder. She raised her arms high to the sky. "Markie!" she yelled. "Pull it in!"

Bo whipped his head around to stare at Mark. Mark's eyes widened. His mouth fell open and Bo almost felt the inhale as whatever Mark did to nullify magic was pulled inward, giving Eden the space she needed.

"STOP!" the little girl screamed. "I want you all to stop!"

A raw wind swept down the street, harsh and strong. Hair blew, clothes flapped. Eden's voice echoed from the building to building.

Stop…stop…stop… The sound went on and on.

Everybody froze in place. In mid-step, mid swing; it all stopped. One by one the balloons popped and faded. The strange impossible animals that walked the street disappeared. Engines from stalled cars fired to life. For one brief moment, Main Street was free from magic.

Dalt gave a funny grunt. In slow, careful movements he stepped around Claire and John. He patted May on her shoulder as he passed her. He stepped in front of Bo and reached up with gentle hands to lift Eden down.

She wrapped her arms around his neck and cried. Bo felt his own eyes tear up as he watched the big man hold the little girl. Dalt's eyes held a look of wonder, as if he held the most precious treasure in the world in his arms.

She raised her head, patted his cheek and said, "Put me down now, Dalt. I'm okay."

He nodded and gently handed the little girl to Frank.

"What now, Dad? We need to get out of here before whatever Edie did wears off."

Too late. The jumpsuits were getting to their feet. The mob began to stir. The soldiers were slow to respond.

Frank ran a hand over his head. "Flicker, can you use magic to clear the road? Mark, as soon as Flicker clears our path, you let out whatever you did to allow Eden to use magic. Once your ability to nullify is back and the road is clear, we're out of here. Hang on tight." He slid back behind the wheel.

Shelly jumped out of the cab and helped Flicker, with the use of magic, to clear the road between the truck and freedom.

Bo and Mark took up positions. Bo put the slingshot to work, taking down the closest of the jumpsuits.

"I wish I'd chosen the sling." Mark slanted a downward look at the leather pouch still bulging with stones. "I'm thinking there is an advantage to shooting from a distance."

"I agree." Bo readied his sling and let fly at the closest jumpsuit running at them.

Frank yelled, and they hung on as the truck moved forward. Flicker and Shelly ran ahead, staying in front of Mark's nullify and retaining use of magic.

"We're in trouble!" Mark called out in warning. "It looks like everybody is going to come at us at once. We'll be overrun by sheer numbers."

Bo was pulling his knife out, prepared for close-in battle with the jumpsuits, when Eden shrieked.

"Look at the sky. Look, look!"

They looked skyward. Bo moved to pound on the roof of the cab. "Uncle Frank, stop. Step out and look. You'll not see this again."

Frank stopped the truck, hopped out, and looked upward.

One by one, the mob stopped moving toward them and looked up to see what had caught their attention. The soldiers looked up. Finally, the jumpsuits halted to look.

Dropping from the sky, looking like some strange flock of birds, came thousands of bodies. Not free-falling as if dropped from a plane without parachutes, but in a graceful descent. At the front, wings spread wide, flew Silas.

Eden recognized him first. She grabbed Bo around his waist. "It's Silas, Bo. He's come back. He's brought the teachers and hunters. They'll save us, Bo!"

The jumpsuits took one look at the bodies dropping from the sky and scattered. Bo figured they knew if they were captured, the fate awaiting them at the hands of the people dropping from the sky would be far worse than simple incarceration.

The mob pulled back. The soldiers looked for their weapons but Flicker was having no part of that. She put another heat spell on them, hotter this time. The weapons melted into a pile of unusable metal.

One by one, the teachers and hunters landed. Silas, recognizing Flicker and the children, strode toward the truck.

The hope of Earth had arrived.

Chapter 31

His round, golden eyes resumed normal proportions as he moved from other-sight to human. A wide grin lit his face.

Flicker ran to him. He swept her up and spun her in a circle, making her laugh. He set her down and greeted the children with humor and enthusiasm. Around them, chaos reigned as hunters, teachers, and volunteers began to touch ground.

Flicker and the children tumbled over their words, getting introductions made to Frank and Claire. Claire gave Silas a frazzled grin before running to catch May and prevent her from trying to catch people descending from the sky.

Frank shook hands with Silas, a form of greeting that clearly puzzled the Hunter. The small group, unable to be heard over the screaming, shouts, and greetings, moved toward the guard shack. The soldiers were trying to restore order, a fruitless effort. Nobody paid them any attention.

"You couldn't have arrived at a better time," Flicker said. "Everything is so confused right now, this is a good time for us to leave. Silas, we've found a place for you to headquarter out of but I can't take you there. I need to make sure the children get back to the farm." She frowned in thought.

Silas, now that the initial greetings were over, looked hard at Dalt. "I see you've caught one of the renegades. I take it he's been judged? Otherwise, he wouldn't be standing here with you."

Flicker, still frowning, waved at Dalt. The big man smiled and waved back at her. The children started to giggle, stopping when Claire frowned in disapproval.

Flicker sighed. "I don't see any help for it, Silas. You're going to be needed here until things get straightened out. I can't stay but somebody needs to." She turned her head and looked at Frank, appraising him.

He nodded. "I know what you're going to ask. Yes. I can take Silas to the nursing home and show him the accommodations. I'll stay long enough to make sure he understands the needs of the community. While everybody is distracted, it's a good time to get out of here. Nobody is paying any attention to us."

Claire started to cry. "Frank, no. I don't want to go home without you."

He went to her and pulled her into a hug. "You have to, Claire. Your parents need you. Get them settled into the farmhouse. Start preparing for winter. I don't think I'll be longer than a week or two. Silas can't know how things work without some guidance. I'm the best person to stay here and help."

"He's right, Claire," Flicker said. "We need to leave now."

Claire pulled back. She nodded her head, wiped away her tears, and gave Frank a fierce kiss.

Silas added, "We have people with us capable of bearing messages. I can guarantee you'll get regular reports."

"Heck." Mark leaned close to Bo and spoke. "Cosmos can just peek in if he needs to."

Bo shrugged. "There is no reason to think Cosmos will be at the farm."

The boys fell silent and watched. Flicker, Frank, and Silas pulled away, spoke in undertones.

"That's it, then." Flicker turned back. "We're out of here. Line up and move out."

Silas and Frank said their goodbyes before heading back into the milling crowd.

Without Frank to drive the truck, they decided walking to the clearing was the best option. May didn't want to leave the excitement of people flying in the air. Eden walked up to her, smiled at her grandmother, and gently reached for her hand. "Walk with me, Grandma." May smiled at the little girl and followed her down the road toward the clearing.

"How does she do that?" Bo wondered. "That's what she does to the pony. She doesn't even need a lead rope on Teddy, and he would follow her to the ends of the earth."

Mark shrugged. "She's a charmer. I'll give her that."

Bo turned for one last look at the town of Grayson. *What a mess*, he thought. *But what a sight. I'll never forget the day it rained people.*

Mark turned around and both boys walked backwards for a few steps.

"Did you ever think you'd see such a sight?" Mark asked.

"No, and I don't think we ever will again," Bo replied.

"Look!" Bo pointed.

A small group of newcomers, talking to Silas and

Frank, broke apart and moved in the direction they had last seen the jumpsuits. One of the newcomers went from two-legged to four. His body elongated and his head went to the ground.

Behind them, making both boys jump, Flicker spoke. "One of the peculiarities of magic are mutations." The boys stopped walking, staring at the small group fast disappearing from sight.

Flicker spoke again, her voice going soft with wonder. "We never know the why of it but magic somehow meets needs. The Hunter who just went to the ground is a specialized breed. He is a Tracker. Frank must have told Silas about the criminals that have escaped. Silas is sending a group after them."

She gave the boys a moment to digest her information, then added, "Come, we need to get around the curve and out of sight of the town."

The boys nodded, turned away from the town, and broke into a jog to catch up with Claire, their grandparents, and the girls.

Chapter 32

Fifteen minutes later, they caught sight of the wagon and the horses. Harley had everything lined up and ready to go.

"Where is Cosmos?" Bo asked his uncle.

"He showed up at the clearing and told me to move everything to the road. He said as soon as we got May and John and the girls loaded in the wagon, I was to send you, Mark, and Flicker to him."

Flicker frowned, giving a quick look at Eden. Dalt lifted the little girl into the bed of the wagon. The little girl laughed at her grandmother, daring the old woman to climb in with her. Answering laughter looked good on May's face. For a split second Bo saw an eerie resemblance between his grandmother and his little sister.

Dalt, a big grin on his face, grabbed May around the waist and lifted her high before setting her gently in the wagon so she could sit beside Eden.

It took Dalt, Harley, and the boys working together to get John and the wheelchair into the wagon. Flicker and Eden added a push of magic to lighten the load.

Shelly wanted to go with the boys but Flicker told her to stay with the wagon. Even though Hemlock had been caught, there were criminals on the loose. Shelly would be needed if the wagon came under attack.

"We won't be long, I promise," Flicker assured the girl.

"I don't want to go at all," Bo protested. "I've seen Cosmos render judgment. Heck," he lowered his voice and said to Mark, "I've felt it. I don't want to be anywhere close when he does it to Hemlock."

Flicker waved Harley off. "Go. Don't worry about us, we'll catch up to you before nightfall. Probably even within the hour. Don't stop for any reason."

Harley nodded, and clucked to the two horses pulling the wagon. The other two horses had been left in the clearing. Once Hemlock was squared away, Bo, Mark, and Flicker would ride the remaining horses to catch up. The little pony, Teddy, was tied to the tailgate. Eden sat in the wagon as close to the little pony as she could manage.

"Let's go," Flicker urged the boys. "Cosmos will be wild if we don't hurry. He's been after Hemlock for a very long time."

Flicker called out a warning as they neared the clearing.

"Cosmos has probably been watching us anyway," Bo said.

Flicker frowned at him. "Calling before you enter a camp is a courtesy. One you'd do well to remember." She shook her head. "I forget how much knowledge happens from living, how much you have yet to learn. Hunters live by rules, Bo. Respect, manners, these are simple things and will stand you in good stead."

She fell silent before stopping. She turned to look at them, her eyes serious and probing. "Never forget that magic can be harsh. You've seen how I flick in moments of danger? I don't choose what I do. My body reacts, usually before my brain registers the danger. Magic chooses for me. If you surprise somebody, they may not wish to harm you but the magic will act before the brain can think. Courtesy is safer."

Bo and Mark nodded.

"Ho, the camp!" Mark yelled.

Bo added, "We're coming in, Cosmos."

Flicker grinned.

Cosmos, using some means of light not identifiable, had the clearing so bright no shadows from the trees and shrubs were discernable.

"Geez." Mark held a hand up to shade his eyes. "What's going on?"

Cosmos, eyes still lava red, made an impatient sound and cranked the light back a few degrees. Hemlock lay huddled on the ground.

Bo frowned at the dejected huddle on the ground. "I don't picture Hemlock as being a crier." He spoke softly to Mark.

"Me neither." Mark's expression matched Bo's. Both boys stood looking at the old woman.

Flicker came to stand beside them. Although older than the boys, she wasn't any taller. They stood, shoulder to shoulder, frowning at Hemlock.

"Have you questioned her yet?" Flicker asked Cosmos.

He spoke, his anger evident in the stiff tone of his voice. "I have not. I felt it best to have witnesses before I do anything to her." Both eyes showed volcanic eruptions. "I am not rational at the moment. Justice dictates that I render a fair and impartial judgment."

"Yeah," Mark murmured for Bo's ears only. "I can see how impartial Cosmos is right now."

"Shh," Bo shushed his cousin. Without thinking, he put some distance between him and Mark. He stopped when Cosmos turned a red-eyed gaze on him. "Um, what do you need us to do?"

"I need you to witness judgment. If you stand over there," Cosmos pointed to a group of trees and shrubs, "you can watch without being touched by the light."

Bo didn't hesitate. He headed for the designated 'watch spot.' Mark and Flicker followed hard on his heels. None of them wanted to risk being caught when Cosmos unleashed the 'Light of Truth.'

"I still think she looks weird." Mark stepped a few feet outside the 'safe' spot. Bo grabbed his arm and pulled him back. "She does, Bo." Mark looked at Flicker. "What do you think?"

Flicker leaned to the side, peering around Bo and Mark. She eyed the old woman huddled on the ground, sobs shaking her frail body. Flicker straightened back up, her eyes going thoughtful. "Maybe we should talk to Cosmos."

Too late. Bo swallowed whatever he'd been going to say and hit the ground, curling up into as small a ball as he could manage. Mark and Flicker did the same.

A flash of light lasting no longer than a flash bulb on an old-fashioned camera lit the air. Bo raised his head, crawling forward just far enough so he could watch Cosmos pull the black cloth back over his head, effectively cutting off the light that comprised his body. Bo rocked back on his heels, coming up to a half-crouch.

"I must say, that was… disappointing." He looked outraged when he swiveled his head to look at Mark and Flicker. "I'm sure Eden and I were in the light for at least fifteen minutes. How does that old woman get off with a nano-second?"

"Shh," Flicker warned Bo.

Too late. Black-clad legs stood next to him. As Bo looked upward, Cosmos seemed eight feet tall. Cosmos reached down and hauled Bo to his feet. Mark and Flicker were already standing.

"Are you shaking?" Mark leaned closer to Cosmos, a puzzled frown pulling his eyebrows so close together they almost met in the middle.

"I am." Bo hadn't thought Cosmos's eyes could reflect a deeper anger than the erupting lava. He was wrong. Cosmos's eyes revealed something so dark and primal Bo couldn't look at them.

Flicker flicked, appearing by Hemlock, a fact that shocked her so badly she flicked again, appearing on the far side of the clearing. Bo didn't know who to watch. Cosmos, in his rage, or Flicker, overcoming her nerves to stalk across the clearing back to their side, or Hemlock, lying huddled on the ground.

"Somebody tell us something," Mark burst out. "I want this over with so I can go back to my parents."

"That woman." Cosmos spun away from them and strode to the woman. Even without looking, she felt his presence, and shrank away from him.

"Not you." Cosmos sounded disgusted. "I pity you. It's Hemlock I'm angry at."

Flicker, Mark, and Bo exchanged wide-eyed looks before they ran to Cosmos.

"What do you mean? This is Hemlock." Mark pointed at the old woman.

"She is not." Cosmos sounded like he was speaking through clenched teeth. "At the height of the chaos, when everybody was coming at us from every direction, Hemlock performed an unspeakable act."

He looked down and finally the anger left his eyes, replaced by gray rain. A soft, mournful look. He knelt down on one knee and lifted the woman up. He cradled her in arms that offered comfort. Bo watched him stroke the old woman's hair with a gentle, soft touch.

"I am sorry." Cosmos spoke softly to the woman. "You have suffered enough. We'll take you to the farm and I promise when we find Hemlock, she will return to you what she took."

Mark looked puzzled. "What is he talking about? Flicker, can you explain to me what happened?"

The woman nodded. "I think what Cosmos is telling us is that Hemlock is no longer wearing the body we know her by. She has stolen an identity. I would bet money this is a woman at the prime of life. When Cosmos emitted the burst of light and the sonic boom stopped everybody in their tracks, Hemlock timed her switch perfectly."

Cosmos rose to his feet, the woman cradled in his arms. "I saw what I was supposed to see. This woman was unconscious. I thought I had caught Hemlock. Instead, I left the scene and Hemlock has faded into anonymity. We don't even know what she looks like anymore."

Bo's stomach tightened in dread. "We need to get back to the wagon. Nobody knows this yet. Eden is in more danger than ever before."

Cosmos nodded. "I agree. I'll take this woman to the

wagon. You get the horses and ride. I want everybody back at the wagon within the hour."

Cosmos ran a gentle hand over the woman's head one more time, this time putting enough magic into his touch to put her to sleep. Cradling her gently, he rose into the air. As soon as he cleared the tree line he flew away.

"Let's go." Flicker ran to the horses. Mark scrambled onto the saddle of the buckskin. Flicker leaped onto the back of the appaloosa. Bo tried to get up behind her but the horse kept sidestepping.

"Hold him still, Flicker." Bo stood, red-faced and angry.

"I can't." Flicker shook her head. "You come at him too fast. I'll stand him in a ditch and you can get on from the side."

And that's what they did. The ditch Flicker chose was deep enough that all Bo had to do was grab onto the back of the saddle and do a little hop. He was on. He had barely settled himself when Mark and Flicker kicked the horses into a canter. Bo held on for dear life.

Chapter 33

Bo didn't want to think about the last two weeks. The woman who looked like Hemlock was still with them. She told them her name was Serena and she was nineteen years old. Frank, Claire, and his grandparents were still staying with them. They hadn't yet moved into the old farmhouse.

Silas and Frank arrived in the middle of the night, waking everybody up and setting off a joyful reunion. As they talked, Bo realized an astonishing amount of work had been done in the town of Grayson.

Teachers and Hunters were teaming up and being dispersed throughout the contaminated area. It was hoped they would be able to educate the populace about what could be expected in the upcoming months and to help people prepare for the winter. Children were the hope of the world. If they could be taught how to live in a world full of magic, the transition period from mechanized world to magical realm would be made easier.

The kitchen was full to the brim with people. Silas rose to his feet, his golden eyes bright with laughter. "I have an announcement to make."

Everyone fell silent.

Silas's smile widened to a grin. "It has been my pleasure, over the last ten years, to have as my apprentice Flicker." Everybody looked at the young woman. She turned pink at the attention. For a few seconds, her body flickered wildly before she calmed down and held her ground. "Flicker has been a model student. Diligent, hard-working, and careful to learn her lessons well."

Bo and Mark started to grin. Bo leaned closer to Mark and whispered, "I think I know what's coming."

"Me, too." Mark slid off the counter he'd been perched on and stood up.

Silas went to stand on one side of Flicker. Cosmos moved to stand on the other. Cosmos handed a box to Silas. He opened it and pulled out a green ribbon with a silver medallion hanging from it like a pendant.

Silas slid the ribbon over Flicker's head. Bo leaned forward, squinting to get a better look. "Hey, that looks like an owl."

Silas nodded and his smile widened. "It is. Every Hunter has their own symbol. Mine is the owl. If you see somebody wearing it, you know they trained with me. I decide when my apprentice is ready. Flicker has earned the right to be a full-fledged Hunter. She will be taking on an apprentice of her own."

Cosmos patted Flicker on the shoulder, leaning in to touch her cheek with his. "And Silas will be taking on a new apprentice."

"Wow." Mark grinned. "When will you find out who your new students are?"

Silas swiveled his head around, reminiscent of the owl he was often referred as, and grinned at Mark. "Cosmos will make that announcement now."

Bo's stomach fluttered. "Uh oh." He hastily wiped his hands on his jeans.

Cosmos's eyes went summer blue, and puffy little clouds appeared in them. "I'd like Shelly to come forward."

Shelly grinned and went to stand in front of Cosmos. He put a hand on each of her shoulders. The summer blue vanished, replaced by the sharp hawk eyes, piercing and bright. "Shelly Tanner, it is my pleasure to apprentice you to Flicker, to begin training to be a Hunter."

"I thought I'd be a Teacher." Shelly beamed. "I didn't think I'd get to be a Hunter."

Flicker nodded. "You may very well become a Teacher but Earth is going to need every Hunter it can get. I won't lie to you. The transition period is going to be hard. Until the change is complete, chaos will reign. Hunters will keep the peace."

Cosmos spoke again. "Eden Tanner, will you come forward?"

Bo heard his mother start to protest. He gave her credit for stopping before Eden heard her.

Eden stepped up to stand beside Shelly.

Cosmos knelt to bring his face to her level. "Eden Tanner, will you join your sister, Shelly, in training to be a Hunter? Flicker will take you both on as her apprentices." He stood up and walked to Ed and Grace. He placed hands on Grace's shoulders. "Due to Eden's age, we ask that Flicker, Shelly, and Eden use this house as their base. I would not ask you to turn your daughters away from your supervision. I only ask that you allow them to be trained properly, without interference."

"Thank you, Cosmos." Grace didn't attempt to stop the tears running down her cheeks. "I can accept the necessity of training if they stay here. I understand it has to be done but thank you for not taking my daughters away from me."

She turned away from Cosmos, burying her head against Ed's shoulder. Ed blinked hard to clear his own eyes, before nodding his head in agreement.

"Who is going to be Silas's new apprentice?" Mark burst out. Bo, watching Cosmos's eyes, stepped back when he saw the gray fog. Gray fog usually meant Cosmos was going to say something unpleasant to hear.

The gray lightened, showing a hint of rainbow. "Come forward, Mark Cooper." Mark grinned and hurried to stand in front of Silas.

Cosmos put one hand on Mark's shoulder, and the other on Silas. "Silas, it is my pleasure to turn Mark Cooper over to your instructions."

"Wait a minute." Mark stopped Cosmos. "I can't do magic. How can I be a Hunter when I can't use magic?"

Cosmos turned his head and met Mark's gaze. "We don't know yet what you can do. Silas job is to teach you the rules a Hunter lives by. You will need these skills regardless of whether you can access magic or not. Every adult human must learn the rules. Silas is also going to work with you to find out how this ability you possess works. It is new to us. We are going to be learning from you as much as you're learning from us."

He turned to look at Frank and Claire. "I know that you and your parents are going to be inhabiting the old farmhouse. In deference to your needs, I ask that Silas and Mark be housed with you."

"That goes without saying." Frank nodded.

Bo took another step back. The noise of questions being asked, feelings being expressed, grew to uncomfortable proportions. Without thinking, he put his fingers in his mouth and let loose the loudest whistle he could manage.

Silence. All faces turned toward him. He stared at Cosmos.

"What about me? You haven't told me what I'm supposed to do. Do I get to be an apprentice?" Bo's stomach tightened even more. Surely, he wasn't going to be left out.

"Yeah," Mark added. "What about Bo?"

Cosmos held a hand up, stopping the noise once again.

"I haven't forgotten you, Bo Tanner. Step forward and accept your mission."

Bo strode forward, stopping in front of Cosmos. He looked up at the taller man, noticing Cosmos's eyes had turned a startling color. One he'd never seen before. A color of energy, hope, and strength.

"For the first time ever, Bo Tanner. I find myself in need of an apprentice. Will you accept the position?"

Bo gaped. "You? I'm going to be trained by you?"

Behind the black cloth, Bo saw Cosmos's mouth tilt upwards. "If you accept this position, then yes. I will train you to be a Hunter. I find myself in need of a companion who can help me navigate this world of yours. Will you accept the position?"

Bo looked around at his family, and his new friends. He looked back at this strange being known to him as Cosmos. His stomach, knotted so long with tension, filled with warmth. He grinned, nodded his head. "I accept."

Chaos reigned as shouts, laughter, and celebration began. Life on Earth would never be the same again. Let the world of magic begin.

About the Author

    C.L. Roth is an artist, caregiver, and author. She started her writing career writing articles for her local newspaper. A job that taught her to write tight and meet her deadlines. She is a full-time caregiver for her son. Joshua was born with cerebral palsy. He is a talented watercolor and acrylic artists. C.L. manages OurHome Studio which showcases her son's artwork as well a rare pieces of her own work. She manages two websites: www.clroth.com and www. ourhomestudio.com.